The Stone Boat

# The Stone Boat

A. V. DENHAM

ROBERT HALE · LONDON

First published in Great Britain 2003

ISBN 0 7090 7508 1

Robert Hale Limited
Clerkenwell House
Clerkenwell Green
London EC1R 0HT



2 4 6 8 10 9 7 5 3 1

Typeset in 11½/13½pt Sabon by
Derek Doyle & Associates, Liverpool.
Printed in Great Britain by
St Edmundsbury Press, Bury St Edmunds, Suffolk.
Bound by Woolnough Bookbinding Ltd.

I know where I'm goin',
And I know who's goin' with me.
I know who I love,
But the dear knows who I'll marry

Anon. Folksong.

Are we compatible?
Wanted to walk the Camino to Santiago
for mutual support and companionship
like-minded pilgrims/travellers.
Start St Jean-Pied-de-Port mid September.
Contact Jon for initial meeting in London.

The advert appeared in a Saturday edition of *The Times* & *The Daily Telegraph* one week in May. It listed an 0181 telephone number. It attracted something over twenty-five replies.

# Chapter One

'You'll be good for Grannie Margaret?' Rebecca knelt in front of her six-year-old son to re-do his trainer laces. There was a small tear in the knee of his new combats, she noticed philosophically. 'You really should learn to tie your shoes properly, Toby,' she scolded mildly. 'One of these days you'll fall and hurt yourself, not just your trousers.'

'We're always good for Grannie Margaret,' Toby replied indignantly, ignoring the rebuke, 'aren't we, Grannie Margaret?' smiling up at her winningly. 'Can we have chicken nuggets for tea?'

'Of course you are always good, my darling, and we'll see,' said his grandmother indulgently. Toby beamed, knowing he'd get his way. 'Now, say goodbye to your mother or you'll never get your tea and she will be late for work. What is Charley doing now?' Margaret Parry, two bulging overnight bags over her arm, returned to the kitchen to find her granddaughter scrabbling in her school bag. 'We must be going, darling. Leave that until Sunday evening.'

'I did a picture for Mum at school. I forgot to give it to her,' and Charley, flourishing a piece of paper, ran past her grandmother and into her mother's arms. 'Look, Mum. This is you at work.'

'Whoops,' Rebecca regained her balance with difficulty. 'It's great. Though I don't think my stove looks quite as messy as that.'

'It does when Hilde cooks.'

'Well, thank you, anyway. Give me a hug and I'll put it on the kitchen board straight away.'

'Me, too, Mum,' and Toby put his still-chubby arms round Rebecca's neck, hugged her tightly, stroked her shoulder-length auburn hair that she had left loose and gave her a sloppy kiss on each cheek.

'Come on, darlings, or the traffic will be dreadful.'

'See you Sunday,' echoing in her head and smiling fondly as the car drove off, Rebecca waved them all goodbye. She sighed. Already the place seemed unnaturally quiet with the children gone. She looked at her watch. Margaret was right. She'd be late for work if she didn't hurry.

The knock at the door came at 5.30 a.m., insistent, demanding to be answered. Rebecca came awake groggily. On a Sunday? She rarely returned home before midnight and the household was used to going on tiptoe until Rebecca had achieved her prescribed eight hours' sleep. But Charley and Toby were sleeping at Grannie Margaret's because Hilde was having a long weekend, and no one ever disturbed her on a Sunday.

Dragging a cardi long past its prime over her knee-length T-shirt, Rebecca stumbled downstairs. The doorbell was chiming at regular intervals now and as she reached the hall the knocker thudded again. 'I'm coming, damn it. I'm coming.' Flinging open the door, 'What the hell do you think you're doing at this hour on a Sun. . . ?' she yelled, and then her heart began to pound and her stomach lurched because in the doorway was no neighbour, or lout looking for a bed to crash in for the rest of the night, but two figures in uniform: two constables – a young man and a middle-aged woman.

Rebecca held on to the door post mutely for the second it took the woman to ask: 'Mrs Parry? Rebecca Parry? May we come in,' holding out her ID card as Rebecca gave a barely visible nod.

'Are you on your own, Mrs Parry,' asked the policeman solicitously, 'or is there, perhaps, someone else in the house?'

Rebecca swallowed. The police only came to your house at this hour to make an arrest or to. . . . 'I'm on my own. The children are. . . .' She stopped. The children. 'Charley . . . Toby . . .

are they? Where are they?' She put both hands to her mouth.

The woman PC said gently, 'I think you'd better sit down, Mrs Parry. There is no easy way to tell you this, I'm afraid. There's been an accident, a fire. . . .'

'Where are they? Are they safe? What—'

'They were dead on arrival at hospital. I'm so sorry. . . .'

Rebecca heard the words quite plainly. They were meaningless. The police might have been communicating in an alien tongue for all she grasped what they were telling her. In the dim recesses of her mind, though, she was aware of a thrumming in her ears, a yawning gulf opening in front of her in which lurked indescribable horrors ready to swamp her. The next few hours passed in a haze. There was tea. It was hot and sweet. Rebecca threw up. The woman stood behind her, saying nothing, her face sympathetic. She handed Rebecca a damp flannel. Toby's flannel. He must have forgotten it. Rebecca sat on the sofa hunched over herself, holding Toby's flannel to her breast as if it were a lifeline. Susan, a neighbour who occasionally baby-sat for them, arrived. The police took Susan to one side. Information was exchanged. Susan, looking stricken and suddenly much older than her fifty-odd years, sat beside her. After a moment when she appeared to debate with herself what might be acceptable, Susan took Rebecca into her arms.

'We'll go now. The children's father will need to come to the hospital tomorrow, you understand?'

'He'll be here shortly.'

Mike arrived as they left. 'Rebecca. Um – Susan. I can't take this in.' He shook his head. Dispassionately Rebecca noticed that his face had sunk into itself. It was almost as if you were seeing his skull as it would be when he was an old, old man. If he, or you, lived that long. Unlike his children. Or his mother. The pull of the pit of despair was almost irresistible. If she succumbed, faced the horrors, it promised eventual oblivion. 'Oh, God,' she said, speaking for the first time. 'I can't bear it,' and in saying it, stepped back from the brink.

As divorces went, it had not been acrimonious. Father of her children though he was, Mike had become impossible to live with. Overriding ambition was one thing, but it played havoc with family life. When they had first met when she was twenty-seven, Mike was already a senior registrar at a London teaching hospital. They had met in Sainsbury's, at the exit. Rebecca had left behind a packet of smoked salmon at the checkout. Mike, unable to attract her attention, had run after her, reaching her at the automatic doors.

'That was very kind of you,' she managed, after she had got over a degree of fright at being grabbed from behind by a tall, personable young man.

'I'm sorry I startled you. But I couldn't make you understand.'

'I thought you were calling after someone else.'

'Smoked salmon, checkout said. Having a dinner party?'

'No. I didn't feel like cooking, that's all.'

'I take it you have a bottle to go with it?'

Rebecca shook her head. 'I only drink with other people.'

'In that case, why don't you let me buy you a drink now so that we can get to know each other better. Then, maybe one day next week you might like to come out to a meal with me? That is, if you think you can trust me after I have introduced myself properly?' He said it so solemnly, she could only laugh and agree.

'Except that I am buying the drink. To say thank you.'

That the two had ever got together after the first meeting was something of a small miracle, let alone fall in love, start an affair then decide to share a flat. Rebecca was a chef in a prestigious restaurant. It had not mattered that their hours were incompatible, that she worked until late and always on Saturdays. They loved each other. Then the children came: Charlotte unplanned, but after the initial shock they decided they were delighted and that they should get married. Toby arrived two years later because by then they had not wanted an only child. There was a succession of nannies and au pairs to enable Rebecca to get back to work as soon as possible. Like most young married couples in the same circumstances, they needed both salaries to fund the help they required for their children and lifestyle. It could have been a treadmill, an energy-sapping grind except that Rebecca found enormous satisfaction in her work and Mike aimed to become the youngest consultant in the shortest possible time. And in the beginning they loved each other. Before it went sour. There were none of the blazing rows Rebecca understood from friends in similar situations were to be expected; there was no overt infidelity – on either side. There was just indifference, a polite coldness that in its way was worse, and finally the acknowledgement that they could no longer live together.

The one good thing about those months before they decided to part was that Mike felt the same. The children were to suffer as little as possible. They would live with Rebecca and see their father frequently, which was when Margaret Parry, herself a widow, became such an essential part of their lives. And now Grannie Margaret and Charley and Toby were gone.

The fire had started in Toby's room. They suspected matches, an inquisitive little boy playing with something he knew he should leave alone. They had a coal-effect gas fire at home, but Grannie Margaret used a wood burning stove and matches. Rebecca had heard her say to the children on several occasions that matches were dangerous. None of them smoked so there was no other reason for reiterating that fire could burn, could kill.

Except that it had not been fire that had killed them all but smoke inhalation. It killed quickly, they said. All three were found in their beds suggesting that unconsciousness overcame them before they even knew they were in danger. Was that really true or were they just telling her that to spare her, Rebecca asked herself? To preserve what semblance of sanity that remained in those first awful weeks, Rebecca went along with it. They had died painlessly. The images of grief persisted: the two tiny, white coffins beside the more solid adult one; Growler, the stuffed dog who guarded Toby's bed at home when he went to stay with Grannie Margaret, rendered in flowers and left on the grave; Charley's new flute which she was learning to play; the helpless shock on the faces of her colleagues who had no words that could comfort her and scarcely dared even touch her arm.

Alone – Hilde had gone to another family – Rebecca was frozen, her hitherto frenetic life suspended as though in aspic, or ice. Lacking the necessary concentration, she had no choice but to give up work. Methodically, because it seemed to help, she stripped the house of all traces of the children except Growler and a teddy of Charley's (her favourite doll had gone in the coffin). She framed Charley's last picture. It all proved too much. Everything was too much. It was Mike, wanting to get shot of the house and all it stood for and disturbed by Rebecca's monosyllabic replies over the phone, who realized something was wrong. He called one evening on a transparent pretext, discovered her in a state of near collapse, unkempt, malnourished, dehydrated. He arranged professional help and she was hospitalized for four months.

She was never once seen to weep. To one of the doctors she admitted that if losing one child was akin to losing a limb, losing two had wrenched vital organs from her body. She could never see herself as whole again.

'It will get easier.'

'I don't want it to get easier. I want them back.'

Like a straw before the wind she went along with the treatment. In time she discovered that the doctors were right in some respects. Sleeping became easier, eating was no longer a problem. She actually became bored and sought something with which to occupy herself. She was taking up valuable bed space that she no longer required, they decided. It was time for her to return home.

Home was the problem. It was no longer a haven, merely a shelter, a shell. It was not even their old house, for the sale of that had gone through quicker than he had anticipated so Mike, wanting visible proof of the end of that era, had rented an unfurnished flat for his former wife while she was still in hospital.

It was Susan, near enough still to visit frequently, who recognized that while Rebecca required time for the healing processes, time on her hands was the worst thing she could have.

'Now that you have the flat as a base you need to get away.'

'You're surely not suggesting a holiday?'

'Certainly not one where you'd have time to brood. You need to do something energetic for several weeks, something with other people.'

'I'm quite content as I am.'

Susan knew when not to press but every now and then she made a remark about getting away, suggested a TV programme featuring an exotic location, or dropped an article into Rebecca's postbox.

'I wouldn't know what to do on holiday,' Rebecca said flatly, one evening when Susan had told her she was looking ill.

'You're either working too hard (Rebecca had taken a part-time job as a receptionist) or you're not sleeping again, or both. Get away. Decide in different surroundings what you are really going to do next.'

'Is there to be a next?'

'Of course you have a future. Don't ever doubt that.'

'Some future, without—'

'Yes, well. Being sorry for yourself won't help,' said Susan abruptly. There was an intake of breath from the woman in front of her and Susan contemplated a ruined friendship. 'I'm—'

'Please don't say you're sorry,' said Rebecca wryly.

'Go away,' Susan persisted. 'Oh, I shall miss you but you need to see fresh places, fresh faces. This, we, everything is too close. You don't have to go away for ever. Just take some time out where people don't know you or what you've been through.'

Anonymity. It had an unlooked-for attraction. 'I've never seen myself trekking in the Himalayas,' objected Rebecca slowly, 'or any of the other Andrex trails,' she added firmly.

'I was afraid you might say that,' Susan replied, 'but I saw this in the paper the other day and I just wondered. . .' She shrugged. 'Well, read it anyway and see what you think.'

Rebecca read the advert, rejected the notion of a pilgrimage before she'd finished the first line, but Susan was aware that she did not give it back and deliberately made no mention that she realized. Two days later Rebecca, passing the local library on the way to work, went in on impulse and found a map of Europe. So that was where Santiago de Compostela was, northern Spain. She did not know northern Spain. She hunted in another section and found something about Compostela. The pilgrimage was known as the Camino. 'Five hundred miles,' she exclaimed aloud.

A middle-aged woman sitting beside her and frowning over the keyboard of one of the library's computers shushed her crossly.

'Sorry,' whispered Rebecca. But, five hundred miles. . . . She'd expire after only a tenth of that distance. Perversely she borrowed the book anyway.

Somehow without her realizing it, the notion of getting away had become acceptable. What occupied her now was where she would go. She tried to analyse what it was about trekking that she had always found distasteful. It wasn't the lack of so-called facilities. It was the enforced bonhomie, walking with a group of people you'd never met before and probably loathed not only at first but at second sight, too.

So you'd get that on a pilgrimage. Some of them would be decidedly odd.

But on a pilgrimage there would be no compulsion even to be civil, if that was how you were feeling. Moreover, Rebecca liked the notion of becoming a traveller. Of course there would be plenty of time to brood, but she was coming to understand that brooding was an essential part of the healing process – perhaps not brooding, more allowing herself time to reflect.

It would do no harm to go along to the meeting.

# Chapter Two

Rebecca hesitated at the doorway of the Cavendish Room of the small hotel on the Edgware Road, took in its motley assortment of occupants with an all-encompassing glance, curled her lip and turned on her heel.

Fool that she was. She should have known better. This was an exercise in total futility. Its only saving grace was that she had not mentioned a thing about coming today to Susan. Her departure would have been swift but unobtrusive if she had not collided with a small greying woman whose capacious handbag was knocked from her grasp, scattering its contents on the floor between their feet.

'Damn,' exclaimed the woman, kneeling awkwardly to retrieve her belongings, making contact with Rebecca's elbow and dislodging the glasses from her nose in the process. Her next expletive was more colourful. 'Ah, sorry about that,' she said, as she righted glasses and herself and grinned up at the slender young woman anxiously looming over her.

Of medium height, Rebecca was stunningly attractive, fashionably thin (too thin), auburn-haired and flamboyantly dressed in black flowing trousers and a tunic top with striking jewellery. (The jewellery was also perverse, making a statement that she wasn't about to walk in rags – if she walked at all.) 'You forget about your language living on your own,' the woman went on, 'and I never did know when to hold my tongue.'

'It was my fault. I changed my mind about the meeting at the last minute and decided to escape while I could. Let me,' Rebecca said, picking up papers, a pristine comb, an ancient biro without its top, an immaculately clean large white handkerchief. They moved to one side while the elderly woman was stuffing everything back. 'Don't I know you?' she asked uncertainly.

The woman gave her a piercing stare. 'The name's Ella—'

'Saxeby,' Rebecca cut in. 'I remember. You live next door to my mother's old house.' Immediately she cursed herself mentally for getting involved. She had a sinking feeling that it would have been so much easier to have just walked away.

'Rebecca. You must be Rebecca. You've lost weight.' Ella quite plainly suddenly recalled local gossip for she went a little pink. 'How are you, my dear?' her tone solicitous.

'Oh, as well as can be expected, under the circumstances. You know, divorced my husband eighteen months ago, lost my mother to cancer a year ago, lost my – my children. . . .' She stopped, turned away. Even to her ears, the brittleness sounded inept.

Ella took her firmly by the hand. 'So it is true. I can't say how sorry I am. It must be absolutely dreadful for you.'

Rebecca made a big effort and turned back to face Ella. 'Yes,' she said simply, her eyes glistening.

'So you saw the advert and thought the Camino might be a good idea.'

'I did. I've changed my mind.'

'Just like that? Don't think you're cut out to be a pilgrim after all?'

'It would be a ghastly mistake.'

'On the other hand,' said Ella, 'you can't really tell until the meeting's actually happened, can you? It's due to start in five minutes.'

For the first time in many weeks Rebecca smiled as another, unfamiliar instinct compelled her to say, 'I'm almost sure I'm not cut out to be a pilgrim, but if you are one of the companions on the road, I might find myself becoming a traveller. I always forget first impressions are very deceptive.'

'Shall we find seats?'

Second impressions in that hotel room were no better than the first. Rebecca became more convinced than ever that the idea was a non-starter. But she had definitely lost the opportunity for escape for the moment. She looked round. There were twenty people. Twenty. Logistically impossible, unless they had bookings ahead. Rebecca hadn't the slightest intention of roughing it any more than was necessary.

'I wouldn't want to walk with such a large group,' Ella said doubtfully, echoing Rebecca's feelings.

But, 'Oh, no you don't,' said Rebecca firmly, clutching at Ella's arm as the older woman began to rise to her feet. 'Like me, you'll just have to wait until it's over.'

'Ladies and gentlemen, friends. . . .'

Jon, whose advert they had all answered, was a spare man with a receding hairline. He had a clear, carrying voice, with a compelling tone which had initially convinced both Rebecca and Ella over the phone that coming to his meeting was a good idea. The man had a persuasive manner too, body language that promised he would be all things to all men as he held out his arms to embrace the assembled company.

It repelled Rebecca. She found she was listening with increasing distaste as, preliminaries swiftly over, the man began listing the ground rules to which his band of pilgrims should agree to adhere if they wished to join the pilgrim group on the Camino.

'Pilgrim?' interrupted a young man with a beard. 'I'd be coming as a traveller.' He glared as if daring anyone to contradict him. Instead there was a ground swell of agreement. The man with the beard subsided.

'There are many reasons for walking the Camino,' Jon answered smoothly. 'Cultural, spiritual, religious. Any of these qualifies one as a pilgrim. I confess that my motives are more religious than cultural but I would not dream of denigrating those of anyone else.'

The muttering ceased.

'Ground rules,' continued Jon, unperturbed. He began listing them: 'leaving in mid-September, staying in pilgrim refuges and moving on every day. . . .'

'What about rest days?' came a reasonable objection.

'If you really need to take a rest day you'd have to move out of the refuge and stay in a hostel or a small hotel. Catch us up. The whole point about refuges is that they are free, or they provide beds for a very small price, though only to accredited pilgrims and just for one night. Or travellers,' he added belatedly. 'Of course, you'd have to be members of the Confraternity of St James. I am.' He expanded on this. 'You'll find leaflets on the table with applications to join. And I need hardly add, you'll have to have membership to get your pilgrim's passport which entitles you to the benefits of the refuges, not to mention the Compostela at journey's end in Santiago.'

'You said for one night. What happens if someone's ill?'

'A good question. Exceptions can be made for one extra night at a refuge but, basically, if you're fit enough to walk, you walk. If you're too ill you have to leave the refuge to be nursed.'

The room digested this information. 'Well, I suppose no one would contemplate this in less than reasonable health,' someone observed. 'And there's always insurance.'

'For the modern pilgrim.'

Someone else guffawed.

'Quite,' said Jon. 'To continue. I vote we have a no smoking rule.' There was no dissent to that. 'We dress, and live, modestly. No alcohol.'

'Come on,' scoffed a man of about retirement age. 'When pilgrimages were really in vogue, I bet all those gourds they carried contained wine, or at least a mixture of wine and water. The non-alcoholic stuff was often far too dangerous to drink. What about the spirit of the age?'

'Rioja,' Rebecca muttered to Ella. 'If he thinks I'd go without that, the man's more of an idiot than I take him for. I'm leaving, just as soon as I can without causing a fuss.'

His voice still utterly reasonable, Jon said, 'True pilgrims, or travellers, usually like to deny themselves some of life's so-called pleasures on a journey such as this.'

The man who had objected to the no-wine rule stood up. 'Look,' he said, 'we came because we really liked the sound of your advert and thought the whole venture worth considering, but I think it's already obvious that we would have nothing in common with your ideals. There's nothing wrong with any of life's pleasures if they're used in moderation. I mean, you'll be banning sex next.'

There was uproar – not all of it anti. 'Refuges do have dormitory accommodation, you know,' Jon said stiffly. 'Intimate relations are quite out of place under those circumstances.'

The man rolled his eyes towards the ceiling. 'Well, I'm sorry if we're in the minority, but I really can't agree with your so-called rules and I think it's only fair that we stop wasting your time and leave you now.' Again there was audible murmur. 'Coming, Posy?'

His wife thus addressed, who was sitting beside him looking quite bemused, got up with alacrity. 'Sorry about this,' she muttered audibly to her neighbours. 'Do please excuse us. Thank you so much,' as a huge plastic Debenhams bag was hauled out of her way. 'So sorry,' she repeated, as she followed her by now plainly exasperated husband. Under cover of the distraction, while Posy and her husband extricated themselves from the middle of the row in which they had been sitting, Rebecca said, 'This is my chance, too. Nice to have seen you again, Ella. Bye.'

When she went to close the door behind her, Ella was there also. 'What an escape,' she exclaimed. 'I should have let you go when you first wanted to.'

Rebecca smiled again. 'Perhaps not. It was all rather fascinating in a horrid way.'

'Wasn't it? Waste of an afternoon, though.' Ella consulted her watch. 'I've an hour before my train. Would you let me buy you a drink? In the interests of partaking of one of life's little pleasures and all that.'

'I believe I saw a pub round the corner,' Rebecca replied.

They ordered gins and tonics and as they went towards a table a familiar voice said, 'More refugees from the companions from hell? Come and join us.' It was the woman called Posy and her husband.

There were introductions all round. The man was Philip. 'Posy,' said his wife.

'I'm Ella,' said Ella. 'Obnoxious man,' she exclaimed, without referring to the him by name. They all knew whom she meant.

'But what a good thing he had the sense to get us all together first,' said Posy.

'I wouldn't be surprised if Jon doesn't have a few takers, all the same,' said Philip, 'and a small group of compatible people is much more likely to stay together on a long journey than the crowd he'd got.'

'My thoughts exactly,' another voice chimed in. 'Room for two more? I'm Bill,' he said as he pulled two more chairs into the circle. 'And this is. . . .'

'Oliver.'

Bill was a good-looking man, tall, well over six feet, with an abundance of well-groomed dark hair and just that distinguished hint of grey at the temples, and a cleft chin. Oliver was not much shorter, younger and more casually dressed – possibly early forties, Rebecca guessed – not conventionally good-looking but with well-cut fair hair, a smile that lit his eyes and a friendly manner. Rebecca was struck by his pallor. She wondered if he had been ill. The two men had been sitting next to each other, she recalled. It occurred to her they might be a couple.

'They say you should never go on a journey with a group without meeting them in the pub first,' Bill was observing. 'I'd say we've got a good nucleus here.'

'Are you suggesting what I think you're suggesting?' asked Oliver.

Bill shrugged non-committally. 'There's nothing to stop us, is there?'

'Nothing except common sense,' interposed Posy. Her husband nudged her arm gently.

'Do you really mean you think we could form our own group?' Ella sounded more excited than anything. Then she hesitated. 'But we don't know anything about each other, do we?'

'I don't suppose Chaucer's pilgrims knew the slightest thing about each other when they first met,' said Bill. 'If they had, do you think they would have joined forces? I very much doubt it.'

'I suppose that's what a pilgrimage is all about,' said Ella, 'travelling to a special destination with total strangers.'

Rebecca said, 'But I don't want to go on a pilgrimage.' Nor, at that moment, did she want to go on any sort of a journey, unless it was on her own when she would have all the time she needed to remember happier times – to brood.

'Not a good idea,' Ella whispered in her ear, 'brooding too much.'

'Not your business,' Rebecca hissed back, not sure whether to be offended or bruised by the accusation. In that moment she changed her mind. Travelling anywhere with Ella Saxeby right now would be fraught with complications.

'Still. . . .' Ella persisted, and said no more.

'Nor do I want to go on a pilgrimage,' agreed Philip into the silence. 'But a journey is something different, isn't it? Don't you think we might travel together on that basis?'

# Chapter Three

For a long moment there was no evidence that anyone agreed with Philip's suggestion that, looking on the Camino as a journey, they might join forces and travel together.

'I think another round is indicated,' Oliver said, as it looked as though the group was about to disperse through sheer inertia. 'Same again?' He went to the bar.

'Personally I've gone right off the whole idea, pilgrimage or journey,' Posy announced unhurriedly, smoothing the stuff of her fine heathery-tweed skirt across her knees. 'Not that I was ever very keen to start with.'

'You are, of course, speaking for yourself, dear,' her husband rebuked her mildly. 'The idea still has immense appeal. It was just those absurd ground rules that threw me.'

'Quite,' agreed Bill, after a small pause.

'We'll talk about it later,' Philip added, in an undertone to his wife.

Feeling more sympathetically disposed towards Posy than Philip, Rebecca wondered if pomposity were catching. Then Philip said with a grin, 'Then you can throw something at me, Posy dear.'

Looking round the group, Rebecca suddenly had the distinct impression that Bill was about to say something significantly different. That maybe his idea of leadership was more closely akin to Jon's than they realized. She lifted her chin, challenging him as if she really minded. Bill's face remained unruffled.

'Are you seriously suggesting that the journey could go ahead after all, with the group here?' Ella asked Philip.

'Why not? We all came to the meeting with just that in mind. So, Jon and his cronies are not the companions for Posy and me, but that's not to say the rest of you aren't.'

Ella said slowly, 'I had hoped to start nearer the beginning of September. Say, the first or second from St Jean-Pied-de-Port.'

'What about accommodation?' asked Rebecca. Someone had to be devil's advocate, she was thinking. 'I suppose I wouldn't mind using refuges if necessary but I'd prefer a little more privacy and comfort to a dormitory.'

Bill said, 'There's a book called *A Practical Guide for Pilgrims* which gives plenty of good advice. It lists every inch of the Camino, with accommodation.' He reached into his briefcase and passed the guide to Oliver. 'It wouldn't be too difficult to book ahead, so building in rest days at good hotels.'

'I wouldn't go otherwise,' Philip said unexpectedly. He squeezed his wife's hand as if in further apology.

'Are you all right for your train?' Rebecca asked Ella, mindful that she had not been exactly polite to the older woman.

'I think I might miss it. This is becoming too interesting to leave.'

'Forgive me,' Rebecca said quietly and compounding injury, 'You must have thought about distances, the rigour of the journey. . . .'

'At my age? I'm sixty-nine, if that's what you're asking.' The reply was defiant, loud enough for everyone to hear. Then Ella sighed. 'Well, actually I'm seventy-one. I can still do an average of ten miles a day.'

'It's twenty-six kilometres, over sixteen miles, from St Jean to Roncesvalles,' Oliver said unexpectedly, passing the drinks round.

'So when I get there that'll be my first rest day,' declared Ella.

'And mine, too,' said Posy. If I come, was a plain, if silent amendment.

'I also understand that some pilgrims take public transport from the industrial outskirts of the larger towns to the centre,' Ella continued impassively. 'You can probably count me in for the bus. In fact I doubt that I shall be walking with you all that often, since I'll have fallen behind. I shall see you when I see you.'

'Would that be safe?' asked Oliver anxiously. 'I'm not sure you, or any woman come to that, should think of walking on her own.'

'On a pilgrimage?' scoffed Rebecca, her tone suggesting it would be an audacious man who messed with her.

Oliver shrugged his shoulders. 'In my opinion,' he said stiffly.

'I probably won't walk alone,' said Ella. 'As I said, there's always a bus or some sort of local transport.'

'Well,' said Bill dismissively, 'that would be entirely your own decision.'

Oliver grinned a little maliciously at Rebecca. 'Time's not really an object for me,' he said. 'Walking with people I like is.'

She sensed he disapproved of her without understanding just why. There was a time when Rebecca would have bristled, even knowing all too well that there were men who claimed that red hair spelt trouble. Nowadays she had no energy for that sort of sexual sparring. 'If you and Bill think you'd prefer to be with only really strong walkers, perhaps you should say so now.'

'Oliver and I aren't a couple,' interrupted Bill frostily. 'We met at the door of the pub.'

'Pulled inexorably,' said Oliver humorously.

Oops, thought Rebecca. She'd got that one quite wrong. And there was a diplomatic apology to make, too. 'I'm sorry Ella,' she turned to the older woman. 'I didn't mean to sound insulting. I daresay you are a stronger walker than I am. It was just that I. . . .'

'Felt you had to be honest? Well, I always have called a spade a spade. And at least it sounds as though you have decided to come with us.'

It meant no such thing, but Rebecca thought she had better not say so then. 'I think it's my round. Same again, everyone?'

After that third round in the pub – and it was by no means the alcohol that decided it – the decision to walk the Camino together appeared unanimous.

That meeting with Jon put Rebecca right off any suggestion that she should even take a holiday, let alone have anything to do with the Camino. Rules, indeed. Then, anything as long as the

Camino promised to be would mean leaving the place where her children. . . . Rebecca blotted the picture of the graves out of her mind. She was not in the habit of visiting the cemetery with any regularity, just dropping by when she felt the need. Even then she found absolutely no communication there. Rebecca was really not sure about the afterlife. Whatever, she was comforted by a certainty that her children were safe. It was just that there was this harrowing misery that their safety had nothing to do with her, their mother.

Unfortunately – or could it possibly be fortunately? – the informal gathering in the pub made her realize that not only had she become very intolerant of other people, she was likely to make a most uncomfortable member of a group. After all, what right did she have to question Ella's physical abilities? Philip, she considered, would probably be a reasonable travelling companion, but personally she doubted if Posy would stay the course. Bill might be a pain if he assumed the leadership. She did not know what to make of Oliver. Rebecca shrugged inwardly. She supposed she could stand him, if they mostly walked apart. Not an auspicious way of thinking about those who might be her companions for several weeks. Weakly she allowed the group to believe that she would be joining them, already wondering how she could best extricate herself from a situation she was sure would be disastrous given her state of mind.

Yet the seed that Susan had planted had taken definite root. Nine months had passed since her life had altered irrevocably. Nine months of a mourning that would never entirely go away. But Rebecca did know that she needed to pick up at least some of the threads of her life. There was the small matter of how she was going to live. Like most people she needed to earn her living. There was the question of where she would live, for there was also the beginnings of a conviction that, for her own sanity, she must leave the place that was alive with so many memories. So where would she go? When would she go? What would she do?

It all seemed to hinge on that small seed. Become a traveller for a definite period. Use the time to make decisions. If she could only find the energy to make that first decision.

It was another little thing that clinched Rebecca's decision to go on the Camino. She was walking through Harrods' food department when she stepped sideways to avoid a collision with a heavily-laden American and found herself face to face with a tall man who looked vaguely familiar.

'Rebecca. It's good to see you.' To her surprise, Oliver actually sounded as though he meant it.

Flustered, she said, 'Do you shop here often? I'm looking for dill and can't seem to see it anywhere.'

'I think it's over there. How are your arrangements going? For the walk, I mean,' Oliver said, when he saw the guarded look on Rebecca's face. 'Look, have you time for a cup of tea?'

With the pot of Lapsang between them on the table together with a plate of buttered teacakes, Rebecca steeled herself to confess.

'Not coming with us? Why not? Um, sorry. Not my business.'

'I just. . . . I'm not . . . I want to do a walking trip, I don't think I'm cut out for anything quite like the Camino. It seems a bit intense,' she ended lamely.

'Intense as in the religious thing?'

Rebecca grimaced. 'I'm not sure.'

'I do see that walking for five weeks with strangers you might not necessarily like could be a total bore, but you take that risk going with any group.'

'Of course you do. I realize that. But it could take six weeks.'

'The Camino is certainly different.' He went on persuasively, 'If you really hated walking with us, all you'd have to do is wait for a day, or even catch a bus and go on ahead, which is what Ella said she would do.'

'So Ella is still going with you?'

'She's set on it. Game woman, that one.'

'A bit foolhardy, if you ask me,' commented Rebecca. 'I remember my mother saying . . . oh well.'

'You know Ella?'

'Not really. My mother was a neighbour. She had a lot of time for Ella.'

Oliver noticed the past tense. He did not comment on that but said instead, 'I don't think you should be too hard on anyone, however elderly, who decides to take on what seems a rash enterprise.'

Her cheeks flushed. 'Except for the fact that it might have repercussions on the rest of the group.'

'Granted, but that's life.'

Rebecca's eyes narrowed as she replied, 'Which, of course, you know all about.'

Oliver's eyebrows shot upwards. He was about to make a cutting rejoinder when he saw, or thought he saw the glimmer of tears in Rebecca's eyes. Not something he could challenge her about on a second meeting. He said instead, 'As much as many, possibly not as much of the worse side as some.'

'I'm sorry. I shouldn't have said. . . .' Suddenly she remembered that when they had first met Oliver's skin had an unnatural pallor. It was quite gone now and he looked as healthy as anyone else. Quite healthy enough to undertake the Camino. Her remark, however, might well have been totally inappropriate.

'Apology accepted,' he interrupted quietly. 'Eat your teacake. It's getting cold.'

Rebecca pushed her plate to one side. 'I'm not hungry. You have it.'

'Thanks. You know, the Camino is the one walk where your time really is your own. As Ella says, if she can't – or doesn't – feel like walking one day, she'll take a rest. You could always do the same.'

'With Ella?'

'Perhaps not,' Oliver conceded with a grin, 'but you might find someone you get on well with in one of the refuges. Or even walk entirely on your own.'

'Provided I called in regularly?'

Oliver grinned in appreciation of a point scored. 'It isn't as if we have all vowed to stay together the whole time, have we?'

'I suppose not,' Rebecca agreed reluctantly.

'Do think about it again. And in the meantime have another cup of tea.'

Cursorily she wondered why he seemed so keen that she should be one of the group and why she was having third thoughts. It was possibly that there was something comforting in having someone, however peripheral, concerned about your welfare.

Which was how, if not why, Rebecca came to the little hotel in St Jean-Pied-de-Port to await the arrival of five total strangers as August gave way to September. She was jobless. She had said a final goodbye to Toby and Charley (a fact which she would never tell a soul). She had also bought herself a small gold locket, unlikely to be the object of theft worn inside her shirt, into which she placed with tender fingers the portraits of her dearly-loved children. She was about to spend six weeks doing something the reason for which she had not been able to explain to herself, let alone anyone else and convinced she was all sorts of a fool anyway.

# Chapter Four

Walking the Camino from France to Santiago had originally been Philip's idea. Philip Brockenhurst was an accountant in one of the more affluent Hampshire towns. He was a few weeks off retirement when he saw Jon's advert in *The Daily Telegraph*. It was something of a revelation that this was exactly what he wanted to do. With the prospect of a nice lump sum coming his way to add to the shrewd investments he had made over the years, he and Posy looked forward to prosperous golden years until ill health circumscribed their declining days. The problem, as he saw it, was just how was he going to occupy himself until then.

The advert seemed godsent. Philip was a believer – he supposed. He went to church two or three times a month, walking from his house the half-mile down the road, picking up the Sunday papers on his way home. He went at Christmas, at Easter and for Harvest Festival (he loved the old-fashioned hymns they sang rousingly on that occasion). In his time he had even done the right thing by the PCC by being a churchwarden. A pilgrimage seemed a bit over the top, smacked altogether too much of Anglo-Catholicism. But a walk, one of the great walks of Europe, called him irresistibly. Golf had given Philip a good pair of legs. A long distance walk, call it what you will, would give him time, breathing space to decide what he was going to do with his good years. The distance did not worry him – nor, naturally, did the prospect of carrying a backpack – he was one of the few players at his club who steadfastly refused to use a trolley. All he had to do was to convince his wife that she would enjoy it, too, because it never even occurred to him to leave Posy behind.

The meeting in London with Jon had been worse than anything Philip had imagined. His heart had sunk the moment they had entered the room, but they were a bit late and it was not possible to turn and leave without attracting too much attention. In the end, of course, that was exactly what had happened, sitting on the only free chairs that were not in the front row. But he'd made the right decision, no doubt about that. No way could he have walked five miles with a man like Jon.

Philip had accosted Ella and Rebecca in the bar on impulse. Somehow everything else had happened as if it were meant. He was not too sure about Bill. He had a vague idea he'd met the man before somewhere. His memory being what it was, it was as likely to spring into his mind as not, so he promptly forgot the notion. But Oliver, now he seemed a good chap to have along on a journey.

Philip thought he knew Posy inside out. They had, after all, been married for thirty-five years. Inevitably Philip understood Posy far less than he believed.

'There isn't anything of yours for the Camino in the spare room yet. When are you going to start preparing for it, dear?' he asked her one afternoon in mid-August. He had been retired since the end of July and was very much still at the wandering stage.

'No point. I'm not going.'

'Not going? But you must. I'm counting on you. I can't go without you.'

The conversation, and others like it, occurred over several days until Philip finally understood that Posy meant what she said. Her quiet but adamant refusal to walk the Camino was a devastating blow.

'But why not?'

'I told you after that dreadful meeting that I'd changed my mind.'

'I didn't really believe you.'

'I know, dear,' she said sadly. 'You very often don't listen to what I'm saying.'

'That's not fair. Besides, it's too late to pull out now. You'll have to come.'

'Philip, you're still not listening to me. I don't want to walk the Camino. If you'd decided to do a two-week walking holiday, I'd have come with pleasure. But that distance is just too much. Either you go on your own or you give up the idea.'

'What will you do instead?'

'Probably not very much. Get the house in order. Do some babysitting,' her voice trailing.

'I thought you were going to cut down on your babysitting. If you come away. . . .'

'I know, if I walk the Camino they'll have to get used to being without me. Actually, I might go on a few jaunts.'

'Jaunts?' said Philip suspiciously.

'Jenny suggested we might spend a few days in Florence.' Jenny was Posy's divorced sister who lived in a nearby village and whom she saw frequently.

Philip disapproved of Jenny. He suspected his sister-in-law had a bad influence on his wife, encouraging her to spend far too much money on her clothes – though he had to admit that the result was charming for Posy always looked good, whether it was wearing jeans and a shirt or something dressy. 'Shopping,' he said gloomily.

'Probably not. Maybe the odd thing,' Posy grinned, knowing exactly what was running through Philip's mind. 'But now that you're retired and we won't be doing so much entertaining I really don't have to bother about clothes.'

The comment more than startled him. Philip was well-known in the district. He had a number of business contacts. He believed implicitly that the wheels of society were well-oiled under the benign influence of good food and fine wines in an ordered atmosphere, which it was his wife's mission to provide, and which Posy had done willingly, her dinner parties anticipated by their guests with great relish. All this, of course, took time and effort, he realized that. 'I thought you enjoyed entertaining.'

'I do. In moderation. But I'd prefer to give just supper parties for our real friends in future.'

He digested this. It portended change and change had always unsettled Philip. Which was why he needed Posy with him on this journey. He tried to explain.

'I do understand, dear. But now that you've retired life will change. You have to decide how you'll spend your time. We both have to.'

'It sounds to me as though you've done a good bit of that already.'

'Maybe I have, but it's more a question of what I don't want to do at the moment. You can spend every hour of every day doing good, or learning something, or being cultural. Too exhausting. Maybe a few weeks apart will help us both adjust. And you can always telephone me.'

Philip flew to Biarritz where he stayed one night, allowing himself a modicum of luxury, 'Putting myself in a holiday mood,' said Philip to Posy, over the phone.

'Just so long as you don't get cold feet.'

He deliberately misunderstood her. 'Overeat? I most certainly won't. And if I'm ever tempted, think of all that exercise.'

Then he caught a train to St Jean-Pied-de-Port at the foot of the Pyrenees. The town's houses had white walls set off by stone quoins, picturesque, narrow cobbled streets leading off the main thoroughfare. The hotel where the group had agreed to meet was well-appointed. As he entered, the first person he saw was Bill.

'Good, you're here at last. Where's your wife?'

Philip explained. He was annoyed that Bill seemed more relieved than anything. 'It's probably just as well she decided early on. It might have been inconvenient to realize she had to give up if we were in the middle of nowhere.'

Philip wanted to protest that Posy was not like that but Bill was saying, 'We're just opening a bottle to celebrate. Come and join us when you've got your room.'

The hotel manager was welcoming, the porter insisted on manhandling his backpack into the lift. The room had a view over steeply pitched slate roofs to the mountains beyond. He got out of his boots and washed his hands, as he did so catching sight of himself in the bathroom mirror. Not bad looking, when all was said and done. In his prime, so to speak. Cold feet? Not at all. He could not wait to get started.

The others were sitting a little self-consciously round a table, glass in hand, when Philip joined them, looking he thought, for all the world as though they would rather be anywhere than where they actually were. His heart sank again. To bolster his courage he took a large gulp of a very pleasing white Rioja and almost immediately his spirits lifted. If the wine continued to be of this quality the Camino was going to be as good as he'd always hoped it would be. He remembered Rebecca telling them that day in the bar that she intended sampling the local wines and he raised his glass to her.

'We thought we'd eat together tonight,' said Bill, 'to give us a chance to get to know each other and discuss a few things.'

'Not rules,' said Ella involuntarily.

Oliver chuckled. 'I should hope not.'

'No,' agreed Bill, a little doubtfully. 'Anyway, I'm told there's a very good restaurant round the corner. Though I'd need to book.' There was general assent. 'I suppose everyone has a pilgrim passport?'

'What's a pilgrim passport, Bill?' asked Rebecca.

'The certificate you should have obtained from the Confraternity of St James to prove you are a bona fide pilgrim,' he answered sharply.

She shrugged. 'I don't have one. Am I a bona fide pilgrim, anyway?'

'We said we'd arrange this before we came,' he replied, teeth gritted in annoyance. 'You do realize without it you won't get into any of the refuges.'

'Is that such a big deal?'

'It might be, depending on whether you want a bed for the night or a ditch.'

Rebecca was reminded of a conversation she'd had with Susan who had insisted on vetting her luggage, suggesting the best quality walking gear, the uncrushable silk skirt she was wearing and the dreaded sleeping bag.

'Your own sleeping bag will feel a lot nicer than the straw mattresses offered by the refuges,' Susan had said practically.

'Straw mattresses?' Rebecca echoed faintly.

'And perhaps you'd better practise with that backpack,' Susan suggested.

'How do you mean, practise?' Rebecca frowned.

'Get used to it by carrying it round the house. Put a couple of bricks in it and go up and downstairs a couple of times a day.'

'You're not serious.'

But Susan was, and eventually Rebecca did. And afterwards Rebecca disposed of several make-up bottles in favour of a tube of sunblock thinking philosophically that the rest was only vanity, after all. Unfortunately she'd never mentioned the pilgrim passport to Susan or unquestionably that would have been in her possession weeks ago.

Oliver was saying diplomatically, 'I've read it's possible to get a passport here in St Jean. One of the books mentions a Madame Gautier at the Pilgrim Office.' He looked at his watch. 'Why don't we see if we can find her, Rebecca? I imagine the porter can tell us where to go and there should be time before we eat.'

Oliver and Rebecca went to find the porter. The man indicated a small alleyway. 'Turn left at the top,' he said. 'Madame Gautier is on the left. You can't miss her house.' He hesitated, then said kindly to Rebecca, 'You mustn't mind her manner. Sometimes she can be a little – how shall I put it – fierce?'

'Good heavens,' said Rebecca, as they crossed the road, 'was he being serious? I can do without a fierce Frenchwoman on top of an imperious Bill.'

'Bill's not so bad, really.'

'I suppose you're right. And I know he's very efficient. We probably wouldn't be here without him. I really had forgotten I was supposed to sort this passport out at home. It was because I was in two minds about coming at all, I suppose.' It was all the pressures she'd had. 'You do realize it was you who finally talked me into it?'

'Oh yes?'

'When we bumped into each other in Harrods. I told you I

had decided it really wasn't for me.'

'I'm glad you changed your mind,' he said, with more politeness than gallantry.

'I wonder if I shall feel quite so grateful in a few days?' Rebecca retorted, sensing indifference. 'Oh well, it is good of you to come with me now. My French is a bit rudimentary, so if this Madame Gautier doesn't speak any English, I shall be at a distinct disadvantage.'

Madame Gautier was to be found down a dark, narrow corridor. Her office was her living room and contained a plethora of papers, books, statues and artefacts to do with the Camino. A bright-eyed woman of indeterminate age and authoritative personality, she guarded pilgrim rights with a vigorous and jealous determination that they should not be breached by modernism. 'I regret, but it is quite out of the question,' she said firmly, already turning away. 'There are too many people nowadays who think it is a novel idea to undertake the Way of St James for a scenic holiday. That is entirely the wrong attitude for pilgrims.'

Rebecca was torn between a strong determination not to be thwarted and her original conviction that the possession of a pilgrim passport was no big deal. Then she remembered what Bill had said about sleeping in a ditch. She apologized humbly for putting Madame to such trouble and attempted to explain how her application for the passport in her own country had slipped her mind.

'And why are you undertaking the Chemin?' demanded Madame Gautier.

'Um . . . well, you know, the usual things,' said Rebecca, floundering over her reasons for undertaking what the Spanish called the Camino.

Oliver interrupted smoothly, 'Mademoiselle's reasons are the same as mine, I believe, spiritual and cultural. Is that not so?' Rebecca nodded in relief. 'We have decided to walk together but Mademoiselle had not realized she would need the passport to enable her to stay in the refuges.' Madame looked even more dubious. Oliver took his own certificate out of his pocket. 'The others have theirs. It would be most kind of you if you could give one to her.'

'Others?'

'A small group,' said Rebecca.

'How many?' demanded Madame Gautier.

'Three more.'

'Three? That makes five. That is a large group. There may not always be room for you all in the refuges.'

'We understand. We are prepared to use hostels and hotels,' Oliver assured her.

'And you are walking?'

'Oh, yes,' answered Rebecca.

Madame Gautier appeared to hesitate. Then she said, 'Your English Confraternity is a very important one. You should have joined there. But . . .' she hesitated, made up her mind and smiled kindly for the first time. 'I suppose it is all right.' She reached for a pilgrim passport and proceeded to fill it in with Rebecca's name. 'It will be a fine day, tomorrow,' she said. 'You go up, over the mountains?'

'We're taking the scenic route,' said Oliver.

'Straight up,' said Madame Gautier complacently. 'It is hard, for maybe four kilometres, but better than following the road.'

# Chapter Five

'Wow,' said Rebecca to Oliver, as they returned to the hotel. 'Thank heavens you were with me. I feel taken through a wringer.'

Oliver laughed. 'You don't look it.'

'And why make such a fuss? It's only a walk, for God's sake.'

'Madame Gautier plainly doesn't regard it quite like that.'

'No,' said Rebecca soberly. This walk, or whatever, was already turning out to be more complicated than she had ever imagined. She ached for home, even with its memories. 'Well, thanks for your help,' she said, making an effort which was not lost on the man beside her.

'Oh, she wasn't that bad,' he said. 'Madame Gautier,' he added as Rebecca seemed not to understand. 'You feeling all right?'

'Yes. Yes, I'm fine. Thanks,' she answered hurriedly, not deceiving him in the least, she realized with a feeling of panic. 'At least that's the first hurdle over,' she added to distract him. 'And what do you think she meant about going straight up? I thought we went over a pass.'

'There are two pilgrim routes. One more or less follows the road but I'm sure Bill'll want to go up into the mountains. No doubt we'll find out later.'

The food at their chosen restaurant, excellent and beautifully presented and the wine that flowed copiously, helped to oil the wheels of what might have been a difficult initiation to companionship so that the conversation never flagged. It was not a late night, though. They were all conscious of the long day ahead and by half past ten they had settled the bill and drifted to bed.

They took the Route de Napoléon from St Jean-Pied-de-Port to Roncesvalles rather than following the road over the Valcarlos Pass. 'It's longer,' Bill had pointed out during dinner, 'but the views will be fantastic provided the weather holds and whichever way we go we have to do a certain amount of climbing. It'll be far more pleasant away from traffic.'

'I agree,' said Rebecca. 'But Madame Gautier made it sound as though the path was almost vertical out of St Jean.'

'I gather she sends all the pilgrims that way. According to my map there is another footpath with not such a steep ascent. They join after about three kilometres and it'll be a much easier start for us.'

They met at the church of Nôtre Dame after breakfast. Ella left her backpack with Oliver at the door of the church while she went in to light a candle. 'To pray for the success of our venture,' she said.

'Are you going to do this all along the route?' Oliver asked curiously.

'Maybe where it feels right,' she answered cryptically.

'Do you believe in all that, the candles and stuff?'

'I'm not sure,' came the honest reply.

'You mean if there isn't a God it doesn't matter and if there is you might as well be on the safe side?'

'I wouldn't put it like that at all,' answered Ella. 'I go to church every Sunday. Have done all my life. That doesn't mean to say I agree with everything my particular church states. However, to get back to the candles, I'm not a Roman so it has to feel right before I light one. There are places nowadays where you just switch on a row of little lights. I'm sure it is far cleaner and there's no fire hazard, but it doesn't have the same symbolism as a naked flame.'

'I suppose not.' Oliver had not entered a church for years except for weddings and the funeral of his grandmother. When he had applied for his pilgrim passport he had entered 'spiritual and cultural' as being the reasons for his journey. He was looking forward to the medieval stained glass in León cathedral and the baroque splendour of Santiago itself. For the first time it now occurred to him that visiting the smaller churches on the route – for cultural purposes – might assume a rather more spiritual significance.

He was brought back to the present by Bill who was pointing out the bridge over the River Nive which would take them to the Porte d'Espagne and the exit from the *haute ville*. 'A check,' Bill said. 'We've all got something for lunch and plenty of water? Then let's go. But let's agree to stop on the hour. Call it a water stop, if you like. We'll regroup and see how we're doing. We shouldn't have any problems if we follow the footpath signs, but if those in front are in any doubt, wait for me. Once we're actually on the Camino, there should be even less difficulty.'

'Famous last words,' said Oliver, grinning at Ella. 'There's always some idiot who goes charging ahead and gets it wrong.

'That's not likely to be me, at any rate,' she answered. 'I think my place is bringing up the rear.'

It was a beautiful morning, almost a cloudless sky, crisp and with the promise of heat later. Within a short time they had spread out, with Oliver and Bill in front, Philip and Rebecca in the middle and Ella behind.

'This is where we find out if Bill really is a leader or just someone with an inflated sense of his own importance,' Rebecca remarked, as a particularly steep slope flattened to a gentle incline and she took a deep breath of relief. 'Let's wait for Ella.'

'What do you mean? That sounded a bit severe,' Philip said, as Ella joined them, breathing easily, he observed – though it was early in the day.

'Well, this is the problem with us, as I see it,' Rebecca answered. 'We've come together out of nowhere, so to speak. We've not elected Bill as leader, nor is he being paid to do the job as he would be if we were on a package tour of some sort. He has taken over the right of decision making. We might not all want to go along with it.'

'We could always just leave the group if we objected to his leadership,' Ella said unexpectedly. 'Though don't get me wrong. At my age, I'm much happier walking with other like-minded people. It's just a question of how like-minded we are – not to mention the small matter of my stamina. Have a sweet,' she said, digging into her pocket and producing a packet of barley sugars. 'I am beginning to sound as if my blood sugar is running low.'

'At least you've come prepared. Thanks. That never occurred to me,' and Rebecca accepted the sweet gratefully.

'I take the initial complaints back,' said Ella, as they rounded a bend in the road and found the other men waiting for them, backpacks at their feet. 'He's stopped on the dot. Do I have time for a rest?' she inquired as they drew level.

'Of course. We'll take five.'

Ella Saxeby read *The Times*. She never read the *The Sunday Times* considering that too frivolous nowadays for the sabbath, but on Saturdays she read *The Times* from cover to cover and it was on a particularly wet Saturday afternoon when it was impossible to get into the garden and she felt in need of a little relaxation that she came upon the advert. She read it through once, then again. Then she dismissed it and read a very good article on dividing irises. But during the next few days the advert kept coming into her mind. After the third time it had happened she searched for the discarded copy in the shed, found the relevant page and cut the article out and was immediately very cross with herself. So much so that she screwed the cutting up without reading it and threw it into the bin. Two hours later, she retrieved the crumpled scrap of newsprint, a little damp, but still legible, and shaking her head at her own absurdity, she placed it under the tea caddy.

The Camino. One of the few books Ella had enjoyed at school was the Prologue to Chaucer's *Canterbury Tales*. When Nevill Coghill's modern translation had come out as a Folio Society book she had even bought it and had subsequently read the bawdy stories on winter evenings with considerable relish.

At church the following Sunday the vicar referred to St James in his sermon – why Ella was never to remember – for she heard not a word after the mention of the saint's name, for it sent her back to the advert, to Santiago, named after him. The vicar shook her hand as usual at the church door and was somewhat surprised that she did not fix him with one of her steely glares and comment on a fault in the logic of his sermon. It was a little game they played. Sometimes he even slipped in something especially for her to tear to pieces. Today Ella said not one word. He did hope she was quite well. Not that he actually dared to ask. You did not make personal remarks of that nature to Ella Saxeby. But he thought he might call on her in the next day or so, just to check up. After all, she was getting on a bit and you could not expect a razor-sharp mind as well as a healthy body at her age.

Born in the house in the little village in Kent where now she lived alone, Ella had been one of the village stalwarts for many years, a founder-member of their local branch of the WI and a deliverer of meals-on-wheels for the WRVS on a round that included several frail recipients who were younger than herself. Her parents had died within two years of each other, some ten years previously, leaving her the house, its large garden and a small legacy. The house was becoming increasingly dilapidated but the garden continued to be as productive, and as beautiful, as ever it was in their lifetime. Ella's father had been a schoolmaster of the old type: gentle, scholarly, but not very good with the more rowdy older boys in the village school where he had been head teacher for thirty years until he retired. Ella's mother became a semi-invalid in her forties – much as Ella imagined Victorian ladies had been a century before. So instead of going into the Sixth Form (which she would have hated) or getting a job when she left the Grammar School in Ashford after she had taken her School Certificate, Ella ran the house, cared for her father and nursed her mother. Too young to take part in the Second World War, she had still, as soon as the Dig for Victory campaign started, taken over the garden. Then after the war Ella earned pin money from the surplus produce she was able to grow – though then her only help was a lad – and which she still sold at the WI stall in the market in Ashford on Fridays.

The Camino. If she had been one of Chaucer's medieval pilgrims living in London or even coming from the north of

England, would she have walked to Canterbury, Ella asked herself? Or would she have ridden like the Prioress? In those days how you travelled, once you had decided to go on pilgrimage, was probably a matter of status. Think of the state of the roads, too.

The Camino. It was a strange story, beginning in the ninth century. St James, it was said, having been successful in spreading the Christian message outside the Holy Land, decided to go to Spain. His mission there was a failure and he returned to the Holy Land to be beheaded in AD 44, his body thrown to dogs. Two of his disciples gathered his remains and took them to Iria Flavia in Galicia – *Finis Terrae* – in a stone boat. The relics were not actually identified until 814 when Bishop Theodomir was guided to them by a star, and a cult was born. During the Crusades when the road to Jerusalem was closed to pilgrims it became fashionable to walk the Camino to Santiago de Compostela along the so-called 'milky way' – stars again. Forget it, Ella told herself. You are no believer in cults, nor ever have been.

The vicar duly called, and over a cup of tea and a chocolate digestive biscuit Ella found herself discussing pilgrimages in a general way.

'I've never really considered the matter,' said the vicar, who was very middle-of-the-road. 'Can't imagine myself undertaking anything like that. Well, I mean, Veronica wouldn't entertain the idea for a minute.'

So, Mrs Vicar having dismissed the idea, he would give it up tamely. And they wondered why she had never married, Ella thought dispassionately. 'No, I suppose it wouldn't be Veronica's thing at all. But what do you really think about pilgrimages? Are they of any practical value?'

Only Ella would think first of the practical side, the vicar thought, suppressing a smile. 'I daresay they are of no practical value at all. I mean, think of the blisters.'

'You can buy really good boots nowadays.'

'Um . . . yes, I suppose you can,' never having thought about it before. 'Then, a pilgrimage would take several weeks.'

'At least.'

'At the very least. Depending on where you were going. You'd have to shut up the house. Get someone in to feed the cat. And what about the garden?'

'Quite,' agreed Ella. 'And you could only do it if you were retired, or were a student, or were able to take time off work. Most impractical. Have some more tea?'

He watched while she poured him a second cup. He accepted a third biscuit. 'So where were you thinking of going?' he asked.

'I? Whatever makes you think I. . . .'

'Come off it, Ella,' he said affectionately. 'I know you better than that. Or I thought I did. I never took you for that high church, though. Walsingham, is it?'

'Walsingham.' The word came out explosively. 'Certainly not. You know how I disapprove of all that "them and us" mentality.' There was a pause while the vicar munched his biscuit audibly. 'The Camino.' She said it so quietly he almost didn't hear her.

'The Camino? All the way to Santiago de Compostela? Goodness.'

Ella handed him the advert. 'Not all the way. From the French side of the Pyrenees.'

'Still quite a walk.'

'Yes. So what good would it do me?'

'If you can't answer that, I don't imagine I can.'

'It's absurd, isn't it? At my age. Not even knowing why the idea appeals. And with all the difficulties you've pointed out with the house, and the cat, and the garden. Quite ridiculous.' But he noticed that the newspaper cutting that had plainly been crumpled before was not screwed up now but was carefully smoothed and placed on the shelf where Ella kept her most treasured gardening books.

Ella went to the meeting and was duly horrified by the whole idea. But she rediscovered Rebecca and met Oliver and in a split second decided defiantly that there was time left to her to enter upon an adventure. So she bought the boots and the gear, cutting everything down to the barest minimum. Then she settled her affairs – and talked a neighbour's son into promising to feed the cat – and, because she had never flown and wasn't too happy about the idea, she took the train through France to begin the Camino.

# Chapter Six

When they set off again, the grouping had changed. Philip joined Oliver, and the other three were bunched together until Bill lengthened his stride. 'We've almost reached the one tricky bit,' he said, 'where we actually join the Camino. I'd better just check that we get it right.'

There were two Germans resting at the junction of the two paths with a narrow asphalt lane. Both were carrying huge backpacks and were already looking tired. With a pang Rebecca saw that one of them was wearing combat trousers, just like Toby's. Briefly she closed her eyes to compose herself.

'You all right?' asked Philip, catching her up.

'Just pausing to get my breath before the next uphill section. I do hope I don't look like that,' she added nodding towards the young men.

'You certainly do not,' he said. 'Besides, you're definitely not carrying as much as they are. I bet they ditch a good deal of that tonight. How much will you abandon?'

'I don't see I can abandon anything. What about you?'

'I'm working on it.'

The views of the valley from where they had started were broadening out. Oliver dropped back to wait for Rebecca to catch up. 'Isn't it glorious.'

'Mm. Did you know we are being followed?'

'I would imagine we must be. I expect those two Germans are catching us up by now. Bill said they told him they started the Camino today, like us.'

'Not the Germans. This is a young man on his own.'

'Then he'll probably overtake quite soon.'

At Arbola Azpian the path joined a small road with an easier gradient and they had more energy to appreciate the mountains around them. There were several pairs of Bonelli's eagles – identified by Bill who carried a powerful pair of binoculars and a slim bird book.

'You a twitcher, then?' asked Philip.

'Not really. I don't know as much about flora or fauna as I should,' Bill confessed. 'But I always carry the books when I am walking and I try to remember what I've seen. Look, there's another pair, and another down there. What a sight.'

And the young man was still following them, Rebecca observed in her turn. She was convinced he was not just another pilgrim on the same route. Now he was sitting on a boulder about a quarter of a mile back, waiting for them to set off again. Idly she wondered if Toby would be a walker when he was old enough. Mike had been, apparently, when he was at medical school. Would have been, she corrected herself sternly. Toby was dead. Tears welled. That was the second time today she'd found herself thinking about the children. The whole purpose about this damned walk was supposed to put the past into perspective. She rubbed at her eyes fiercely, fumbled for sunglasses, caught sight of Bill looking as though he wanted to catch her up and put on a spurt. So it looked rude. She could not care less just at that moment. Let him think what he would.

They walked for another five kilometres until they reached a viewpoint where a statue of the Virgin Mary had been erected amongst scattered boulders. A deep valley lay to the south-west. Ahead the road still climbed gently. 'We'll have lunch here,' decided Bill. 'Move off in about an hour.' Philip moved restlessly. 'Does anyone have a problem with that?' Bill demanded, sounding defensive for the first time since their initial meeting in London.

There was no immediate response. The others managed not to catch each other's eyes. After all, it was the obvious place for lunch. Each one chose a comfortable spot, eased off the backpack and sat down thankfully, delving for the provisions they had bought earlier. Rebecca took a deep draught of water and a deeper breath, then she said, 'Bill, I've gone along with all your decisions so far. But as I understand it, we came along as a group of equals. The others might like a say in what we do, where we stop and so on. You must have thought of that?'

Unexpectedly Oliver said, 'Rebecca's right. In a crisis, you'd probably make the right decision faster than the rest of us, but otherwise we'd all like our say.'

'Bill was absolutely right to insist on hourly breaks but I'd like to ask what we do if one of us falls by the wayside?' said Philip. 'And have you noticed that the faster walkers are only separated by a matter of minutes from the slower ones.'

'Me,' said Ella defiantly.

'But anyone can have a sprained ankle, or a twisted knee. What are we going to do then? Abandon the one who is injured?'

No one answered for a moment. 'We're not just on a walk, after all, are we?' commented Rebecca eventually. 'That was really all I came for, the walk. But in a funny way, Madame Gautier made me see it in a different light. I think I'm beginning to realize this is far more than just a walk – though I'm not sure I'd go so far as call it a pilgrimage. Yet,' she added. It might become a catharsis, it might not. That, provided she could steel herself not to drop out, was something she would discover.

'But if we agree to stick by each other whatever happens, the walk could take twice as long as we originally planned,' observed Bill neutrally. 'Not all of us, I imagine, have that sort of time to spare.'

Ella said, 'I would appreciate not being left behind just like that, but I have no intention of slowing you all down. If I can't keep up, for any reason, once you have settled me in an inexpensive hotel you have my permission to leave me there.'

'Perhaps we should have some sort of an agreement,' suggested Oliver. 'To stick together as far as possible and aid each other, if it becomes necessary. And, if you like, we'll make Bill the decision-maker.' There was a murmur of general assent.

'That's good.' The voice of a stranger sounded over their heads. As one, they turned to stare. The young man, who stood behind them as they sat overlooking the view, continued, 'If I go along with what you've just said, can I walk with you?'

'The young man who has been following us all morning,' said Rebecca triumphantly. 'I'm right, aren't I?'

'Yes,' he answered, not meeting her eye but kicking at a stone by his foot.

'You were the one who told me yesterday not to take the steep route out of St Jean,' said Bill accusingly.

'That's right. It's crazy. Everyone does it the hard way, having decided on the Route de Napoléon,' he said. 'No one bothers to look at the map where there is a perfectly good alternative that doesn't involve that awful slog.'

Philip turned to Bill. 'I thought you'd studied the map and come up with the alternative yourself.'

Bill flushed. 'After this young man told me about it, I did look at the map.'

'I don't think it really matters how we came to use it,' said Ella, trying to pacify. 'By the look of those exhausted Germans, we certainly came the best way. And I wonder where they are? I thought they'd have caught us up long before now.'

'They'll not reach Roncesvalles before dark,' the young man said. 'They're carrying far too much weight.' His own pack was even smaller than Ella's. 'I told them there was a better way. They wouldn't listen. By the way,' he said, holding out his water bottle, 'I've run out of water. Anyone got any to spare?'

The group of five hesitated. Water was water, and they had a long way to go and they had all been sweating copiously. Bill said frostily, 'There's a drinking fountain soon after we cross the Spanish border.'

'At the ruins of Elizarro below the collado de Izandorre, I know,' the young man said unexpectedly. 'But I'm thirsty now.' He was still holding out the water bottle.

Ella suggested, 'Why don't we all give him a mouthful. That shouldn't do us any harm, especially if we can refill our bottles soon.' She uncapped her bottle and carefully poured a small quantity into the empty container. 'There,' she said.

Somewhat grudgingly the others followed suit. 'Thanks,' the young man said, and drank deeply. 'So, are you going to let me walk with you?' he asked, when he had finished. 'I like the idea of sticking together. It's what a pilgrimage should be.'

'Some people believe that you should undertake a pilgrimage on your own,' said Rebecca stiffly.

'Well, I did, didn't I?' he countered. 'Then I met up with you. I wouldn't hold you back.'

'What would you have done this morning if we'd inadvertently taken the wrong path?' asked Philip.

'You didn't, did you?'

'No, but what would you have done?' Philip persisted.

The young man shrugged. 'Let you get on with it.'

'Thanks.'

'I wouldn't have known if you were taking a different path on purpose,' he pointed out craftily. 'You came the way I wanted to come. I've watched you. You do the right things, like stopping regularly to regroup. . . .'

'Thanks,' repeated Philip, under his breath.

'I'd like to walk with you.'

'You can't, just like that,' objected Bill.

'Why not?'

'Yes, why not?' asked Ella.

'Well. . . .'

'Course, you have to be careful, making vows on pilgrimage, like you've just done,' said the young man. 'Is that bit of baguette going spare?' he asked Ella, who was carefully wrapping the bread to put it away. 'It'll be stale before long. Pity to waste it.'

Wordlessly she handed it over. 'I suppose you'd better finish the pâté, too,' she said drily.

'Thanks.'

'What do you mean, we should take care making promises on a pilgrimage?' asked Rebecca.

'Well, you know the story about St James and the pilgrims, don't you?'

'Which one in particular? There are quite a few,' said Ella.

'There was a group, rather like you, who started their pilgrimage at St Jean-Pied-de-Port,' he said. 'They vowed that they would stick together through thick and thin. But after the first day, once they'd arrived at Roncesvalles,' – he pronounced it the Spanish way, Oliver noticed – 'one of the group got sick and obviously wasn't going to make it. So some of them started to mutter about it being stupid to have made a vow to stay together and they decided they'd better ditch the sick man straight away before he became a total liability. There was just one who objected. He said it was wrong to make a vow and break it the first time anything went wrong. The others laughed at him for a fool and went on ahead. This one, the one who refused to abandon his friend, stayed with him, carrying the sick man when he became too weak to walk. Eventually, though, the sick man died. The pilgrim still refused to abandon his friend. "I promised I'd stay with him until we reached Santiago", he declared.'

'Phew,' muttered Philip, not quite under his breath. Ella glared at him.

The young man continued unperturbed. ' "I'll keep my vow", the pilgrim avowed. But he also fell ill and the body of his friend became too heavy for him to carry any further. So that night in his despair he prayed to St James. No sooner had he finished praying than he was overtaken by a knight on a white charger who asked him why he was sitting by the roadside with the body of a pilgrim. The sick man told the knight what had happened and the knight offered to take them both up behind him. They rode all through the night and at daybreak, as they approached the outskirts of a town, the knight set them down. The pilgrim, who felt much restored, picked up the body of his friend and continued into the town, but he hadn't gone far when he realized that the town they had reached was Santiago itself. It came to him that the knight on the white charger had been none other than St James. At the cathedral the pilgrim completed his pilgrimage and arranged to bury his friend. It was his intention then, he told everyone who had heard about the miracle, to return home the way he had come and meet up with his so-called friends and tell them exactly what he thought of them.'

'Which was probably quite choice,' grinned Oliver. 'Got any more stories?'

'Some.'

'You have my vote, young man,' said Ella.

'But you should understand that we have several rest days pre-booked at hotels,' pointed out Philip, hostility in his voice. 'What'll you do then?'

'Stay in a refuge if I can. Otherwise. . . .' he shrugged.

'But if you get bored with our company feel free to leave,' temporized Bill.

'Without calling down the wrath of St James,' added Oliver, smiling.

'What's your name?' asked Rebecca.

'You can call me Jonah,' said Jonah.

There was a pause. 'Then, Jonah and everyone, if we're all rested, I think we should get going,' said Bill, getting to his feet with the litheness of practice. At forty-four, Bill might be said to be at the height of his powers, keeping in trim with a weekly vigorous tramp in the Pennines, which he had done for years as he had already explained to anyone who was prepared to listen.

'Just one more thing,' said Jonah. 'I suppose you all chose your stone to take to Santiago?'

'What stone?' asked Philip suspiciously.

'The stone that represents sins committed that you place at the foot of the statue in the cathedral at journey's end.' No one said anything. 'It's tradition,' added Jonah, shrugging.

Jonah and Ella set off while the others were still packing up. 'What made you come on the Camino alone?' asked Ella. With her left hand she turned over the pebble she had picked up surreptitiously and put into her pocket as she shouldered her backpack. Superstition – or tradition – did it matter? It felt right.

Jonah said, 'I'm doing a year out before Oxford. My father said he wasn't prepared to see me sitting in front of the box all summer and he offered to pay for me to go Inter-Railing round Europe. Well, I didn't buy the ticket, did I? I decided I didn't just want to go from capital city to capital city, so I hitched down to St Jean. When we get to Santiago I'll probably hitch further south. Might as well stay in the sun for as long as possible.'

Oh, golden youth launched on to an unsuspecting world, thought Ella. 'Do your—'

'. . . parents know where I am?' finished Jonah with an engaging grin. 'Not really. I said I was heading for the south of France, which I was. I didn't really know how to explain about the Camino. And it's my father,' he said diffidently. 'My mother went off when I was eleven. She and I don't have much contact.'

'I expect she appreciates whatever you give her, though.'

'But you don't actually know anything of the sort,' he retorted savagely.

'I'm sorry . . . no, of course I d-don't.' Taken aback, Ella stuttered. 'It was a stupid remark.' And an awful situation. Such misery was concealed behind that young, untouched face.

'I'd just appreciate it if you didn't go telling everyone.'

'A bargain. That is, I'll not say a word about your mother if you promise to phone your father and tell him where you are. I daresay he gave you a phonecard before you left?'

'You're a shrewd old bird, aren't you?' said Jonah, grudging admiration in his voice, 'but I guess it's a deal.'

'And not so much of the "old bird", if you don't mind. I think we've reached our next turn-off and the others are still way behind. We'd better stop and let them catch up.'

'You doin' all right?'

'I'm fine. And it's more or less downhill all the way from the border.'

# Chapter Seven

It was not downhill all the way from the Franco–Spanish border – a wire fence which they crossed on a cattle grid – to Roncesvalles. They filled their water bottles at the drinking fountain at the ruins of Elizarro and there, while they were resting before tackling the long steady climb up Mount Aztobiscar to the collado de Lepoeder, Jonah dug a tatty piece of paper from one of his pockets and quoted from a translation of the *Chanson de Geste*:

> Taillerfer, the minstrel-knight, bestrode
> A gallant steed, and swiftly rode
> Before the Duke, and sang the song
> Of Charlemagne, of Roland strong,
> Of Oliver, and those beside
> Brave knights at Roncesvaux, that died.

'Good heavens,' exclaimed Oliver, 'my namesake. Who was that Oliver?'

'Dunno,' said Jonah. 'I think he was one of the Twelve Peers. When I was young I used to muddle him with Olifant, which was the name of the enchanted horn which Roland blew to summon help when he was down to fifty men in the battle. Charlemagne heard Olifant but the pagan king, Ganelon, persuaded him that Roland was just out hunting and so they left him to his fate.'

'And Roland is buried at Roncesvalles? asked Rebecca.

'Legend has it,' said Bill, dubious of legend.

*

Oliver was much taken by the thought of his namesake, there, at Roncesvalles, where he would be soon. The Camino, the walk, had until the start of it, meant nothing more to him than something to do while inspiration occurred about his future. In a subtle way its whole meaning had shifted. It was unsettling, but intriguing.

Oliver Cumbernauld had acquired a taste for the good things in life at an early age. Not that at any time had his life been anything but cushioned for his people were landed, lesser county, with a rambling farmhouse, part of which was said to date back to the end of the sixteenth century, still a working farm of a couple of hundred acres on the Welsh Marches where they bred beef cattle, mainly Herefordshires. Oliver, as the first-born son, was to take over the farm which had been built up by his grandfather and, like his father before him, he was sent to a well-known public school which was to be followed by agricultural college. At school, though, his prowess on the rugby field – some might have called it aggression – was greater than in the classroom for, though he undoubtedly possessed a brain, he did not care to exercise this any more than was strictly necessary. It was at this time that he decided that farming was not for him, a lesser disappointment for his parents than it might have been for Oliver's younger brother, Edward, liked nothing more. But one thing and another led to a redbrick university rather than the Oxbridge Oliver secretly coveted. A certain resilience born of his sport persuaded him however to throw off what might have become a powerful setback and he left university with a first in Economics and – more to the point – a job with a merchant bank in the City. It was there that Oliver discovered a passion for figures, their manipulation, how it was done, why it was done, markets and what to the uninitiated might seem like the inconsequential things that influenced them. His subsequent dealings in Futures – contracts to deal in commodities or financial instruments at agreed prices and dates – made his employers a great deal of money, a healthy chunk of which came his way in bonuses.

Oliver was sent to Tokyo. It was exciting, exhilarating; a young man plunged into the depths of a culture that was alien, the natural constraints of home and being among his own kind so loose as to be negligible. At this time Oliver also discovered that he had a natural flair with languages and within a short time he was able to show off passable Japanese – though he never succeeded with the written language – and this endeared him to his local colleagues who were his passport to a wider range of social activities than were many ex-pats.

It was in Tokyo, working as hard as he played, that Oliver reached the pinnacle of financial success with all that came with it, and it was there he almost sank to the very depths of failure. There were still, after several years, occasional nights when he woke with a pounding heart, his body running with sweat as he remembered the risks he had run. Oliver continued to maintain stoutly that he had never done anything illegal. He had undoubtedly sailed very close to the wind more than once. How might it have ended? He knew that there but for the grace of – someone, something – Nick Leeson's prison sentence could well have been his if he had not been recalled to London when he was. It was Oliver's luck that a senior executive had a stroke when he did, that people in key positions were moved around, certain questions were subsequently asked, certain checks made. He had never forfeited a deal but once he was back in London somehow he found himself sidelined. Later the timing seemed almost providential. He lost the support of his superiors just as the Leeson scandal broke. When the inevitable banking redundancies were declared, Oliver was one of the first to go.

At the time he considered this a mere setback; there were plenty of jobs for talent such as his. But as the months passed, contact after contact mouthed insincere apologies for failing to come up with the goods and when even the job interviews dried up, painfully he realized that it was over. Banking had foreclosed on him.

By chance he met an acquaintance from school. Fred was into computer software, he told Oliver. 'I have this package,' Fred said, after a couple of pints. 'An absolute winner.'

Weren't they all? 'So what'll you do with it?' asked Oliver idly.

'Set up my own company. At least I would, if I had the cash.'

And a few weeks later, Oliver was the silent partner in *Wizard Gems* which made exactly the killing in the software world as predicted by Fred. Subsequently Fred, sufficiently headstrong to resent any partner and wealthy enough now to indulge himself, decided to buy Oliver out. Oliver's next investment was a dotcom company. For several weeks he was a multi-millionaire, on paper, until the bubble burst.

It was still not the end of the world. An innate caution – a throwback gene? – had persuaded him even at the height of his wealth not to spend it all. There was a handy one and a half million invested in gilts that would bring in sufficient to live on in less than abject poverty. He owned his London flat and a cottage in Herefordshire not far from his parents that he rented out. He also possessed a Porsche. But the hours of the day were long and aimless.

Oliver only ever used to make occasional visits to his parents. These visits home were generally unsatisfactory on both sides. June and Nigel Cumbernauld had ceased to understand their son once he became a teenager and rebelled against the orderly pattern they had set out for him. They could not understand it then, but they were compelled to regard Oliver as an underachiever. His obvious brilliance at making money since leaving university totally bewildered them. Then the crisis in farming hit them and the absent Oliver was less in their thoughts than the resourceful Edward who insisted long before it appeared necessary that the farm must diversify if they were not to be forced to sell.

Then the end of the world, Oliver's world, became reality. For a number of months he had periods when he felt unwell, suffered headaches. Sometimes he felt dizzy. He went to the doctor. Migraine, it was suggested. Painkillers would probably sort him out. It was just something some people suffered from. No real problem. He shook the tiredness off, had his eyes tested – there was nothing wrong with his eyesight. It must be a migraine. For a while he even appeared to get better. Then the headaches grew worse. Fortunately he was on one of his rare visits home when he collapsed. There were tests, a scan. The diagnosis was a brain tumour.

The operation took place within hours of the diagnosis. It was an apparent success, the surgeon told him cautiously, a benign cyst. Of course, you could never predict absolute success, he amended hastily. There would be sessions of radiotherapy. Just in case. Oliver endured the sickness, the weakness, the loss of his hair. For several months he was convinced his time was very short. Then he began to get better.

He was merely in remission, he believed. The medical profession, still cautious, agreed but suggested the possibility that he might actually be cured. Oliver grew stronger. He began to think there was a future in front of him.

But once more Oliver seemed to have sunk into aimlessness. Nigel would have liked to offer support, counsel, anything, but what was there to give? They thought they had lost him. They still might. They had been so supportive when he was ill. Oliver felt he could never repay his mother for her strength, for those nights when, wakeful, he had gone downstairs, prowling restlessly between kitchen and drawing-room. Inevitably June found him there, made him herbal tea, talked him through the night. Now it was different. He was still their son but Oliver was entirely his own man, self-contained, wealthy enough on his own admission to afford not to work. They did not know how to cope.

So Oliver had reached a crossroads. Lacking a purpose in life, he needed a change of direction. More than anything he needed the incentive to find that direction. It was at this stage that he conceived the notion of going on a journey; not a holiday, but an undertaking that was challenging.

'You're mad,' said June, horror-struck.

'And irresponsible,' growled Nigel. 'What are you thinking of?'

The trouble was, where to go? In no way a mountaineer, he had trekked to Everest's base camp. He had heli-skied in Canada, bungee-jumped in Queenstown, gone ballooning in Tanzania, whale-watched off the shores of Alaska (with a blonde girlfriend who was into wildlife). It had all been frenetic, with too much to do, too much to absorb, no time to think, let alone contemplate the future. 'Not that challenging,' Oliver conceded. 'There are limitations. Besides, you know, been there, done that, bought the T-shirt. . . .'

He'd been at a dinner party, the sort of event he normally avoided like the plague. This night he'd just confessed to the woman on his right – in an attempt to dissuade her from expecting anything to come of the dinner – that he was about to embark on a long journey. 'To take time out to decide exactly where I go from here.' (He was fairly sure that they all knew his background and no thirtysomething woman was going to pursue a man so obviously unreliable, one way or another, in the matrimonial stakes.) Then, pressed, he'd had to admit that the actual journey was still only a vague concept.

The woman on his left became animated. 'A train journey? Like the Trans-Siberian railway? I did that once, during a university vacation. It was fantastic. I wouldn't mind doing it again.'

'Can't sleep on trains,' Oliver replied hastily, in case she thought he might be in need of female companionship on this adventure.

'A safari, perhaps?'

'Watching wild animals for a month? No thanks.'

'Ride a camel across the desert. I've always wanted to do that.'

Suggestions from envious men who had overheard were now coming fast and furiously.

'Too much like hard work.'

'Somewhere exotic by four-wheel-drive?'

'In my state of health I'd probably fall for a debilitating bug,' Oliver shrugged 'Doesn't look as though you've any better ideas than I've had already. At this rate, I might just as well give up the notion.'

'No, don't do that. I saw something in *The Daily Telegraph* only yesterday. Hang on,' and his host left the dining-room hurriedly to return some five minutes later, waving his paper triumphantly. 'Read this.' He watched Oliver's face while he glanced at the advert. 'You didn't spot it yourself? No, take it home and read it again. It might be just the thing.'

It was, after all, the idea of companionship on the road that particularly appealed to Oliver, that sent him to that first, abortive meeting. The Camino was not just a walk, even though it was one of Europe's finest. Nor would it be taken by everyone as a simple pilgrimage. The possibility that this was a true journey excited him, the first time he had been animated by anything in a long time. The disappointment when he understood the calibre of the man who had called them all together was even more crushing. Then he met the others, Rebecca, of whom he was wary even though he had found himself urging her to join them, and Ella. Aged Ella might be, there was something about her that dispelled any sense of the ridiculous that he and she might be companions on the road. And now there was Jonah and his strange stories and they were almost at Roncesvalles, where that other Oliver had been.

'Ella, I've got something for you.' Jonah held out what had not so long before been a long, broken, branch. 'Back there I trimmed this. You've seen that both Bill and Oliver have two high-tech sticks each. On steep stretches they really do help. I know you have brought your own walking stick, but you'll find this extra one gives you greater support.'

'A real pilgrim staff?' said Ella delightedly, hefting it. 'Just like yours.' It was stout, about shoulder height, with a v-shaped cleft.

'Almost,' he grinned. His was gnarled and darkened with age and it curved at the top like a shepherd's crook. 'For a real pilgrim. It might even come in really useful, in snake country.'

'You're having me on.'

'No, though I imagine the chances of seeing one are pretty remote. You know what they say about reptiles being very wary of people.'

'Mm,' she said, eyeing the staff doubtfully. 'That's very kind of you, Jonah.'

'Oh, you know,' he said, scuffing the ground with his toe.

'You were the one who persuaded them to give me water. One good turn and all that.'

'Well, I'll certainly try it.'

'Them, as in four legs, good.'

And then it was downhill all the way, through an ancient beech wood right up to the walls of the thirteenth-century monastery of Roncesvalles and the *posada* where they were to spend two nights. Oliver and Ella followed Jonah to the pilgrim office to have their passports stamped. 'Looking like this, they can't refuse me,' Ella said. She had just about reached the limits of her endurance and was thinking longingly of a bath and bed.

'As if they would,' said Jonah. He arranged to meet the others for dinner and was taken into the refuge where there were beds for fifty pilgrims.

Bill had gone to find out the time of the pilgrim mass. 'Are you coming?' he asked Oliver.

Oliver shook his head. 'I'd rather have a bath and a stiff drink.'

They met in the bar before dinner congratulating themselves that their first day – and traditionally one of the hardest – had been accomplished without any traumas: no injuries, no getting lost, no fallings out. 'Except that we have saddled ourselves with Jonah,' grimaced Philip. He was not sure why but there was something about that young man that irritated him immeasurably. 'I think he spells trouble. At the very least we'll find ourselves subsidising him in some way, if we're not careful. Just look what happened over the water.'

Ella said, 'He's just young. Anyway, I rather like him and he certainly seems to have researched the Camino. I enjoyed his stories. Positively Chaucerian. And here he is,' she said brightly. 'We're just ready to eat, Jonah. Come on, tonight you shall be my guest,' blithely ignoring Philip's raised eyebrows that spoke tellingly of "I told you so".

The next day most of them spent quietly doing nothing more than going into the great church and the chapter house and visiting the small museum.

Oliver was the most energetic, collecting a picnic lunch and tramping in the woods around Roncesvalles, a little disappointed that they were not forging ahead. It was very peaceful. He knew he had done the right thing, choosing to walk the Camino with other people – just in case – but other people could be a strain, and they certainly had been on that first day. Bill was a worrier. Philip was a pompous ass. As he had feared Rebecca was – well, Rebecca was the sort of woman who grated, on him, anyway. It had startled him to find himself offering to help her obtain her pilgrim passport. Without it she might very well have turned back, he thought uncharitably. Then he thought, no, that was the last thing Rebecca would do, give up untried and untested. Then there was Jonah. Actually Oliver agreed with Ella about Jonah, and could you really prevent another pilgrim from joining you for a day or so? Not unless you made it obvious you didn't want his company. Which wasn't exactly the spirit of pilgrimage. Which brought him back to Jonah, and Ella's reaction to the boy. Now Ella he really liked, Oliver decided and he smiled as he thought about her and how he admired her resilience. It was going to be a long journey to Santiago, for Ella. But today it was warm, the sky was blue. The silence that washed over him under the canopy of giant beech trees dappling the leaf-strewn path and forming intricate patterns underfoot, was healing. It was also good to stretch his legs fully when he wanted to. He had begun a training programme once he had decided to walk the Camino. He had swum three times a week and done some weight training. At weekends he walked ten miles. It seemed to have paid off. He was stronger than he had been in a very long time. Only time would tell if it lasted.

# Chapter Eight

After a leisurely breakfast Philip had set about pruning his belongings, whistling his favourite piece of Gershwin quietly as he did so, a sign that he was at peace with himself. Before he had left home, Philip had slipped a slim anthology of modern poetry into his growing pile of must-take; that and a reporter's notepad. Ostensibly it was for keeping a diary. At the back he intended to use the notepad for scribbling. He'd always had a hankering to write poetry. He thought there would be plenty of time for that, on the Camino. At that moment he was beginning to wonder – but there had to be moments of leisure and even if inspiration did not occur he really should keep a diary. Just before lunch he phoned Posy. 'We're all discarding unnecessary baggage this morning,' he told her. 'Well, I am. Ella and Bill don't need to. He says he did all that before we set out.'

'He would. What on earth are you throwing out?'

'Two pairs of socks, underwear, a shirt, the extra towel. I've halved the soap and the toothpaste. And I've ditched the guide-book. . . .'

'Heavens. How dreadfully drastic. Will you manage?'

'I'll just buy new, if things wear out. Bill has a guidebook, anyway. We have a new companion,' and he told her about Jonah.

'That's nice, dear.'

Nice? What did you say to a wife who made that sort of a comment? How banal their conversations had become. Had it always been so or was it this separation that was making it particularly obvious? How did he really feel about his wife? To cover the pause, Philip said hurriedly, 'What have you been doing?'

There was another pause. 'I've been to see some estate agents.'

'Estate. . . . Whatever for?'

'Testing the market,' she said. 'I think I might take a look at some country cottages.'

'Ah. Posy? You won't do anything foolish, will you?'

'Foolish?'

'I mean, we need to talk before you do anything. . . .'

'Foolish?' Posy's laugh came clear down the line. 'Don't worry, Philip. I'm not going to do anything more drastic than go to Florence at the weekend. Talk to you in a few days, mm?'

He shook his head as he replaced the receiver. Wives could be the very devil. What if she. . . ? How absurd he was being. The house was jointly owned. Posy couldn't sell without him. And what if she wanted somewhere smaller, was that so very terrible?

Rebecca was poring over a menu when Philip emerged into the sunlight. 'You look hassled,' she said. 'Come and join me for lunch and tell me all about it.'

Philip and Posy lived in a large Georgian town house with a substantial walled garden which Posy kept immaculate with the help of a gardener. Philip himself disliked gardening, as he explained at length to Rebecca. 'One of the problems I have to face when this is all over is explaining to Posy that it's all a big con, the love of gardening,' he ended some twenty minutes later. 'Oh God,' he said as he saw Rebecca stifle a yawn. 'I've been a dreadful bore. I'm so sorry.'

'Not at all,' she said politely. 'I'm sure you're missing your wife already,' though personally she couldn't imagine why, if half of what Philip said was true. Then she grinned, 'I expect it was the wine we shared. I'm going to have a siesta. See you.'

The days were to acquire a momentum of their own. Almost immediately Philip suspected he was developing a blister and was already regretting one of the pairs of expensive socks he had discarded. Bill had booked in at a private hostel at Cizur

Menor, the other side of Pamplona. Philip's prediction about his blister was right and he said he would find transport to the hostel once they had reached the outskirts of the town. Without much persuasion Ella joined him, declaring that the sights of Pamplona, splendid though they probably were, she could do without. Oliver, however, decided to remain in Pamplona for some sightseeing and to catch them up the following day.

Rebecca was disapproving and told him so. 'It actually has nothing to do with you whether I walk with you every day, or not,' he replied furiously.

'I think it does,' she insisted. 'Once we promised to support each other, we made a commitment to stay together. Here you are, breaking that commitment at the first opportunity.'

'This is ridiculous. All I am doing is spending my rest day here in Pamplona. And if I remember rightly, it was you who talked about calling in regularly. If it sets your mind at rest, that's what I'll do tomorrow night.'

'I don't remember saying anything of the sort,' she retorted furiously.

'Well, you did. When we were having tea together in Harrods. It's Sunday tomorrow. If I'm lucky I might even get to see a corrida. I'll catch you up in two days' time at Puente la Reina.'

Forgetting that chance meeting had been the final thing to persuade her to go on the Camino, she thought he was making it sound more significant than it was. Typically she went on the attack. 'You actually approve of bullfights? You can't see that they are degrading to those who watch them and cruel to the animals?'

He sighed. 'How typical. Oh dear, I might have known you were the sort who'd argue the toss about bullfights.'

'Now you are being insulting.'

Oliver shrugged. 'Yes. I apologize. But I don't propose to go into the rights or wrongs of bullfights here and now. You just have to accept it's a very Spanish thing.'

'I still don't have to like it.'

'I didn't say I liked it. I am still able to recognize that it has its admirable side and I'm absolutely sure that without it the

Spanish countryside would undoubtedly be altered for the worse under the present European agricultural system of subsidies. . . .'

'You're being quite absurd,' she snapped. 'But I really don't want to quarrel with you. . . .'

'Could have fooled me,' he muttered.

She ignored the remark, continuing, 'And what if something happens to you while you're walking on your own? What are we supposed to do then? Break our commitment to you and carry on without checking to see what has gone wrong?'

'Don't be stupid. Nothing is going to happen to me. If it does, I know where to get in touch with you.'

'You would? You promise?'

'Call in regularly, as we agreed. You know, anyone would think you were afraid of leaving me behind for good,' he teased her. 'I didn't think I'd made that much of an impression on you. Or is it just that you want to convert me over bullfights?'

'Don't flatter yourself,' she said coldly. 'I don't and you haven't. I merely think you are being incredibly selfish.'

'Selfish. . . .' But there the argument ended, for Rebecca was walking away, and Oliver was left with the annoying suspicion that either she was perfectly right, or that she had just succeeded in having the last word. Or both.

They were at Puente la Reina with a promised rest day to follow, so there it was that only Jonah disappeared behind the doors of the refuge.

'Glad to see the back of him for a bit,' muttered Bill to Philip.

'I thought you were one of the be-kind-to-Jonah group.'

For the first time Bill looked abashed. 'I shouldn't have said that.'

'I gather he has an unfortunate family. Father left when he was a small child. You know the sort of thing. Quite dreadful, this modern propensity to ditch a husband or wife when the going gets tough. Jonah told me his mother encouraged him to use this gap year before Cambridge to travel and made him promise to keep in touch by e-mail. Amazing isn't it how all the young use cyber cafés nowadays as a matter of course. Are you into that sort of thing?'

There was a slight pause. Bill gave a strangled laugh. 'I don't even know how to programme the video.'

'Not computer literate, then?'

'I can't see the need for the wretched things.'

'You'd be surprised, once you got the hang of it,' said Philip encouragingly. 'Of course Jonah knows all about it, though I'm a bit surprised he expects to find cyber cafés in northern Spain.'

'It's not that I dislike him, you know,' Bill said earnestly, as if to justify himself to himself. 'I just don't feel it is quite right that a young man of his age should attach himself to a group of older people. He ought to be walking with the young of his own age.'

Rebecca, who had overheard Bill's last few words, interrupted, 'And how many of those have you seen? I know there have been a few young cyclists, but the other walkers are either much the same age as we are or they are young couples. I can't imagine Jonah would be made very welcome by them. And anyway, Jonah does his best to entertain us,' she defended him. 'He knows far more about the history of the Camino than any of us.'

'You are quite right,' acknowledged Bill with a tight smile. 'I'll buy Jonah his dinner tonight to make up for my lack of charity.'

Philip snorted. 'There you go, again. Fools, the lot of you.' But it was Bill's way of expressing himself that jangled a few bells in the back of Philip's mind. The reason eluded him. Yet the man was a queer one, and no mistake.

Puente la Reina, halfway between Pamplona and Estella, marks the crossing of the River Arga by a bridge called the Puente de los Peregrinos, humpbacked and one of the most famous architecturally on the Camino. Oliver strode into Puente la Reina around mid-afternoon and came across Rebecca photographing its six semicircular arches and five pillars, each with a spillway.

'Had a good day?' she asked as he was about to pass her with a faint nod.

He hesitated, turned back on his heel. 'Very good,' he replied stiffly. He was about to stride away, paused again, then stopped in front of her. 'I suspect you enjoy walking on your own and at your own pace for a change.' She was trying to be conciliatory, for heaven's sake, thought Rebecca. Just this once, no more. It looked as though she need not have bothered.

Oliver grimaced. 'So you still think I'm a selfish bastard.'

Not the reaction she had expected from him. 'Certainly not,' she retorted, refusing to admit even to herself that there was more than a grain of truth in what he appeared to be thinking. 'As you pointed out, you have a perfect right to walk as, when and with whom you chose. Was the bullfight interesting?'

'Rebecca. . . . Actually, I didn't even check to see if there was one.'

'Good.'

'Did you miss me, yesterday?' he asked daringly.

She was about to deny it forcefully. Then she remembered that she was trying to be conciliatory. 'I think Ella missed you a bit,' she conceded. 'You don't mind walking at her pace. Which is very good of you. But so far as I am concerned, you are now perfectly free to walk as you wish. However, before you go, just stand over there, will you? That'll give me a decent piece of foreground.'

They came to a double-arched medieval bridge at Salado and on the far side Jonah said, 'Aymeric Picaud's *Pilgrims' Guide* contains a story about this.'

'Go on, then,' Ella urged him. 'Tell us.'

*'Take care not to drink the water here, neither yourself nor your horse, for it is a deadly river! On the way to Santiago we came across two Navarrese sitting by the bank, sharpening the knives they used to flay pilgrims' horses which had drunk the water and died. We asked them if the water was fit to drink, and they lyingly replied that it was, whereupon we gave it to our horses to drink. Two of them dropped dead at once and the Navarrese flayed them there and then.'*

At Estella the refuge was newly-built and large. It was also crowded, for a group of Austrian cyclists had arrived shortly before, but they were able to find a corner where six bunk beds were still available. It was the first time they'd had to share with strangers. Rebecca shrugged inwardly as she laid out her sleeping bag on the mattress on the upper bunk. 'I do hope there aren't too many snorers among that lot,' she said to Ella in a low voice.

'They look healthy enough,' answered Ella.

'But you never can tell the state of their larynges by the size of their muscles. In my opinion,' an unaccustomed, unlooked-for giggle surfacing, as she realized Ella was trying not to wonder under what circumstances Rebecca could have gleaned that particular knowledge.

That evening they found a quiet restaurant where they ate a dish of wild asparagus and local artichokes in olive oil followed by chorizo. 'What exactly is chorizo?' asked Philip.

Rebecca said, 'A sausage, of course. Chopped meat mixed with blood and packed into gut. And very good, too. At least, this one is.'

Rebecca saw Oliver, at the other end of the table, lift his glass in a silent toast towards her as if to applaud her definition. Remembering their altercation over bullfighting, Rebecca flushed. Lord, she thought, the man surely didn't expect her to be a vegetarian just because she disapproved of cruelty to animals. Then she lifted her chin defiantly and turned to talk to Bill instead. Ella, a romantic at heart and on the opposite side of the table, sighed. Ah well, the journey was yet young.

As they left Ayegui they discovered a recently installed drinking fountain with a difference. This one dispensed to travellers both water and the local Navarrese wine, which restorative only Ella declined. 'You don't honestly want me to trip over my own feet, do you? Because that's what'll happen if I drink in the middle of the day.'

But in Viana Ella did not feel particularly well; occasional feelings of nausea, the odd bout of dizziness. She ate nothing at midday, just drank a little water. During the afternoon she began to lean heavily on her sticks. Twice she had to stop to turn her face away and heave and bring up the water she had drunk before. Oliver thought she was looking pale and stopped to walk beside her.

'You don't look well. How're you doing?'

'I'm fine,' she insisted.

'You don't look it, you know. Are you sure you're all right?'

'It's nothing, really. At least, I suppose I'm just tired.'

'Aren't we all? But I'd say it was more than that.'

Breathing heavily, Ella stopped. 'I daresay it's the "deadly waters" Jonah keeps warning us against or maybe it was something I ate last night. Perhaps if I'd drunk the wine from that fountain like the rest of you, I should be all right now. As it is, look, I must just . . . excuse me. . . .'

'What do you want to do?' he asked solicitously, when Ella returned from behind a tree looking a little green but composed. 'Stop for a while to recover?'

Ella shook her head. 'I mustn't stop now, but I'm beginning to think I could do with a few days off. In the interest of conserving my strength, you understand.'

'Of course. Look, we'll talk about it this evening, but there's no reason why we can't settle you in a hotel and arrange to meet up later. If that's what you want.'

Bill was disapproving. 'What if Ella is getting really sick?' he asked. Having found an inexpensive hotel for Ella with a patron who was sympathetically disposed towards the ailing and elderly pilgrim, they were eating in a small restaurant. 'We're not going to be able to do anything for her at a distance. Shouldn't we just make sure she goes home now.'

'Now? When she's not stopped vomiting?' exclaimed Oliver.

'I think she's just tired,' Jonah said. 'A day or so in bed and she'll be fine.'

'And what would you know about it, young man?' demanded Bill.

Jonah shrugged. 'I'm just using my common sense.'

Philip put down his knife and fork and said aggressively, 'Jonah's probably right, you know. After all, if you were Ella's age, you'd probably be knocked for six by a bout of sickness.' Bill glowered at him but subsided.

'We can ring her every night,' Jonah continued. 'See she knows where we're staying, just what she has to do to rejoin us.'

'If that's what she wants to do,' said Rebecca.

'She does,' insisted Oliver, who had been the last to leave

Ella's room. 'It was what she called me back to say.' His own bout of ill-health had left him with a residue of sympathy for other people who were obviously suffering. There were small comforts he suggested Ella might require and those not obtainable from her hotel he offered to buy for her.

'As long as we're not reneging on our vow. You know, the one where we said we'd support each other,' said Rebecca awkwardly, and to her own surprise.

They looked at each other for a moment. 'Calling in regularly,' said Oliver.

The others looked mystified. It was Jonah who said, 'I don't think we would be reneging on a vow. Provided Ella is happy about it.'

It was only Bill who looked really dubious.

They went to see her in the morning to explain what they wanted to do. Ella was happy about the arrangement. 'I'll talk to you tonight,' she said, and sank back on to the pillows in such evident relief that she had recovery time ahead of her that they left her without a qualm.

# Chapter Nine

Bill Dyson knew himself destined for the ministry while he was still at school. This in no way surprised his teachers who had always suspected hidden depths in his seriousness and who appreciated the early maturity that did not very often come their way in the boys-only grammar school at which they taught.

The decision delighted his parents who naturally expected that their son would follow the Baptist tradition which had been theirs for several generations. They supported him through university where he read divinity, achieving a good degree, and in the nature of things they would have expected him to continue his theological studies. Then fate intervened in the shape of an uncle who left Bill a small sum of money. The legacy, however, came with the express wish that Bill should take a year out and spend it on travel. The amount was not enough to buy property, too much to reject out of hand.

His parents were horrified by the dilemma. Bill himself was intrigued. It seemed a waste not to accept it – along with the conditions. Yet to become just another backpacker offended his spirit. Bill decided to offer his services for a year as an unpaid helper for a charitable organization that worked, among other places, in the slums of Lima. Why Peru, he was asked by his bewildered parents? When they thought about the idea, which was frequently, they agonized over the dangers. How would he cope? Above all, why Peru? He had a hankering to see the New World, he'd always been interested in pre-Columbian civilizations, he told them. Peru was as good a place as any to fulfil those dreams.

Ah, missionary work, the elderly couple beamed, satisfied,

though Bill's mother did begin to wonder how far and for just how long missionary work would take their son from them.

They need not have worried about him leaving them to become a missionary. The whole travel experience was, quite naturally, an immense culture shock. The poverty appalled him, he had not appreciated how many lived without adequate sanitation. Passionately he declared that he would never, never get used to filthy children, often disease-ridden, begging in the streets. The resilience of some he met to their fate uplifted him to the same extent that the apathy of others depressed him. The gap between rich and poor he decided was obscene – though fortunately the dangerous minutiae of politics passed the eighteen year old by or his tenure of the job might have been ended with barbaric finality, the times being what they were. At the end of his contract, Bill took off for a tour of the pre-Columbian sites that had been one of the reasons he had come to Peru, and it was during these few weeks that he discovered a distaste for missionaries. Convinced Christian though he was, he found the concept of forcing others to a particular belief at the best equivocal, the way it was achieved, iniquitous. Incan gold spent on vast religious edifices made him despair. The suppression of the Incan way of life, the denial of Incan spirituality by a foreign conqueror – for all that its origins were monetary – was alien to his soul.

Bill returned home changed, though at that stage maybe not as radically as some. Not the Baptist ministry, he told his parents. He would enter the Church of England.

So here Bill was, a parish priest incognito, walking as a pilgrim to a place he had no desire to see, in a country in which he had never wanted to travel, and in the company of an assortment of strangers for whom he had little sympathy, with the reason for his being there a hidden secret which he had absolutely no intention of revealing to a soul.

'You feelin' out of sorts?' Jonah asked him. It was mid-morning and for once they had found themselves walking together ahead of the others.

'No. Yes. Of course not, you stupid boy. Anyway, what's it got to do with you?'

Jonah's immediate reaction was to grin irritatingly at the older man and shrug.

*I rest my case* could well have been shouted. Bill flushed.

'I guess we're all a bit worried about Ella,' said Jonah diplomatically.

'Ella should be on her way back home,' said Bill austerely. 'A pilgrimage like this is no place for the elderly and infirm.'

'Ella may be elderly, she's certainly not infirm.'

'My, my, you are her knight in shining armour. I'm sure she'd be most grateful, if she could only hear you, and from her sick bed.'

It was Jonah's turn to flush. 'If you are implying that I sponge off her just because she'd bought me the odd dinner—?'

'Odd dinner?'

'Yes, well, I think Ella is good company and good value. I'd be very sorry if she did decide to go home,' and with that Jonah increased his speed and within a minute or so was several hundred yards ahead.

Bill sighed. Another sin against charity, another display of ill temper. How he'd managed to remain a parish priest for so long considering his current propensity for riling his companions was beginning to seem a small miracle in itself.

Then, in those days he had not thought himself lacking in emotion, unable to empathize with those around him. Had that been the case? He remembered all those interrupted mealtimes when parishioners had telephoned. He had always believed that the judicious utterances he had spoken in times of grief or trouble had been of some consolation. Unctuous? Surely not. You had to try to make sense of bereavement, all the problems that beset folk. Infidelity? There were always the perameters of right and wrong. Perhaps he had merely deceived himself. Was what had happened with his wife the cause of him now seething with suppressed feelings – and some that he could not help himself from uttering?

He did think Ella should give up the pilgrimage now. He did wish Jonah had not latched on to them. He thought that young man was a menace, the type who might land them all into some trouble – though exactly what trouble Bill did not care to enumerate. He also wished that Rebecca and Oliver had chosen to walk with another pilgrim band and that Philip would stop whistling between his teeth. It was always the same tune, too. What was worse, it was unidentifiable.

What he really meant, Bill recognized in the dark recesses of his mind, was that he wished he was anywhere on earth but just where he was.

The refuge at Logroño was newly built and very splendid, reputedly one of the best along the length of the Camino. Over lavish portions of oxtail stew at a nearby restaurant – Rebecca was paying for Jonah's dinner – they were discussing Ella.

'How did she seem?' Philip asked.

'It's difficult to tell really, over the phone,' answered Oliver, 'but she's talking of joining us in a couple of days.'

'Great,' said Jonah. 'I approve of Ella.' Bill raised his eyebrows, but said nothing. 'But she'll miss my stories about Clavijo and I'd mugged them up specially, you know, the battle where St James first appeared as Matamoros, the Moorslayer, astride a white charger. He saved the hundred virgins demanded as tribute by the Moors.'

'Greedy,' exclaimed Rebecca. 'The most I've ever heard requested was twelve.'

'I guess it's the number of wives they traditionally had, harems and all that, so I suppose the Moors always had a grossly over-exaggerated reputation for that sort of thing.'

'Young man, you do have the most extraordinary imagination,' Bill, listening in, expostulated. 'I really don't think you should give rein to it as you do.'

Jonah shrugged. 'The legend's in the books. It's up to you if you want to go along with it. Is there any more of that wine?' he asked Oliver, ostentatiously turning away from the other man.

'No, but you can ask for another bottle, and I'm sure no one will object if you take away what we don't finish,' Oliver said, knowing that Jonah would carry off with ease any apparent social lapse – along with any spare rolls.

Rebecca smiled. She had watched as, inevitably, Jonah pocketed the rolls for his lunch the following day, observing under her breath only that it was a pity the American habit of doggy-bags hadn't quite reached the Camino.

Jonah flashed her an appreciative grin in return. 'I do all right, don't I?'

'Sure. And so do we, though I'm not sure if you have a phenomenal memory or you read the Camino up every night.'

'Bit of both.'

'Thought so.'

'What are you reading next year?' asked Oliver.

'Arabian Studies.'

'Is that why you came on the Camino?'

'Partly,' he admitted. 'I'm gutted by just how strong the Moorish influence remains so far north.'

'And what will you do when you've got your degree?'

'Who knows?' he shrugged non-committally, and a closed expression came over his face so that both Rebecca and Oliver felt not only excluded but as though they had trespassed.

'All right. Tell us another one,' encouraged Rebecca.

'There's a small hill not far away which is either the place where Roland killed Ferragut, the Moorish giant, or the actual boulder he killed the giant with,' said Jonah obligingly.

'You and your wretched legends,' Bill interrupted scornfully.

'You don't have to go along with them. There's more to this one, though. One version has it that Ferragut took prisoner several of Charlemagne's knights whom Roland promised to rescue. They decided to settle the matter by single combat and after several clashes between Roland and Ferragut the giant asked for time to rest. The two then began on a learned theological discussion, finally agreeing that the victor's religion should rightfully be recognized by the other as the true one. As you might expect from a legend, it was Roland who won, but he did so by striking Ferragut in the navel, the giant's Achilles heel which he only knew about because Ferragut had told him himself. I guess at the time they'd both been slightly pissed. Now how's that for fair play? Does Roland still qualify for good-guy status?'

'How very Norse-god,' Oliver remarked. 'I wonder why none of the heroes who confess to a weakness ever expect it to be held against them? It just makes Roland more human to me. I suppose none of us can resist exploiting another's admitted weakness when it comes to it.'

'That's introspective,' said Bill.

'And why not? After all, we are on a pilgrimage, whether we like it or not.'

'Well, I like it,' said Jonah. 'Any offers to buy me dinner tomorrow night?'

They were on their way to Santo Domingo de la Calzada where Ella had promised to meet up with them. There came a parting of the ways: scenic, towards Ciruena, and hilly with it, or following the almost straight road direct to Santo Domingo. Though the scenic route is twice the distance they opted for that.

Oliver set a fast pace. As always, when he was in this mood, the opportunity to cover the ground with a long stride, open his lungs to the fresh, clean air, not to be required to make facile conversation because someone was beside him, gave him a sense of being entirely on his own on the Camino which was renewing. It came, therefore, as a shock to pause at the top of a steep stretch to admire the view and realize that Rebecca was close on his heels. 'Oh, it's you,' he observed ungraciously.

'You needn't sound so surprised,' she retorted, stung by the obvious implication that he'd rather it had been anyone other than herself.

'I'm sorry,' he answered. 'It's usually Bill who paces me and if you want to know I was thinking how very pleasant it was not to have to make conversation.'

Despite herself, Rebecca chuckled. 'Either because you thought no one was there or because I'm not Bill? No, don't answer that. It wasn't fair of me.'

'If I did sound surprised, it was because you haven't walked at my pace before. Actually it's rather refreshing.'

'Thanks. However, I'm perfectly capable of walking without

chattering, so if you've admired the view sufficiently, I suggest we move off. The others aren't that far behind.'

Philip was feeling thoroughly disgruntled. His blister had more or less healed so there was nothing wrong with his feet, but he had to admit that when Oliver got into top gear it was impossible to match his stride. But if he couldn't walk with Oliver, the last person he'd wanted to be with was Bill. The man always seemed compelled to talk, as if it were a duty. Of course, and Philip sighed, it would have been more agreeable to have walked with Rebecca. It had certainly come as something of a surprise to see her keep up with Oliver with apparent ease. Well, he supposed that was youth for you.

'Mm? What was that?' he asked, as Bill drew breath. ' 'Fraid I wasn't concentrating. Look, think I've got something in my boot. Must be careful because of a nearly-healed blister. You go on and I'll catch you up.' And thank God for some peace and quiet, he thought as he sat on a boulder and watched Bill's back disappear round a bend. Mustn't let them get too far ahead, he thought, but this was probably the first time he'd walked more or less on his own and the peace and quiet was bliss. He thought about Jonah, without acrimony, conceding that just maybe the young man did have his place in the scheme of things, smiling to himself over one of Jonah's stories. Fertile imagination the boy had. He'd never have heard anything like that from one of his own sons. Posy and he had three sons. The eldest was now thirty-five. Yes, they had jumped the gun a fraction. But not even Posy realized she was pregnant on her wedding day. All three sons were married. This reflection made Philip frown. Rob, the eldest, had two young daughters. Rob's wife had never worked and Rob himself had just been made redundant, for the third time. Then there was James. James and Fiona had two sons and two daughters. Both were school teachers and as poor (and as feckless) as the proverbial church mice. Finally, and after a bit of a gap, there was Matt. Matthew had done a lot of travelling in his time. He had never had what Philip would have called a proper job. He had been severally a waiter, a chef, a garage hand, a children's counsellor at a summer camp in the States. Currently he and his newly-acquired wife – a stunning

American blonde whom they had yet to meet – were sailing a boat round the Caribbean for its owners. Philip despaired of Matt. Not that he was all that sanguine about the others. Still, there it was. He did so hope none of them were waiting for him to fall off his perch. Neither he, nor Posy believed in inherited wealth. He intended that they should enjoy the fruits of his labours to the full. If – *if* there was anything left when they died, then the children should have it with their blessing. But he hoped they weren't counting on much.

Thinking of the boys, and Jonah who had triggered the reflections off, reminded him: he'd intended doing a bit of writing himself on the Camino beside keeping the diary which he was keeping up religiously. Idly Philip tried to think of a rhyme for pilgrim: grim? Slim? Rim? Him? He shook his head and allowed the silence to wash over him.

# Chapter Ten

Ahead of Philip, Bill was seething in a mixture of anger and resentment. He knew perfectly well that there was nothing the matter with Philip's boot. The man just had not wanted to be civil. Or was too civil to mention that he preferred to walk alone? He lost concentration and almost tripped over a loose stone. You did not have to hold a conversation every foot of the way on a long walk. One of the reasons he'd so enjoyed his weekly walks in the Pennines was for that very thing. He'd not had to converse, in any way, with anyone for a period of several hours. It had been as good as a restorative. At first, Mary had accompanied him on these expeditions but after she became pregnant he went out on his own and somehow they never went back to the old days, even in term times when they were on their own. Mary: Bill sighed, however hard he tried not to think about his wife, thoughts of her intruded. At the age of twenty-seven Bill had decided it was time for him to marry. He chose the daughter of a neighbouring parish priest. Mary, three years younger, knew from experience all about parish life. Together he was convinced they would make a good team and from her response, Bill was equally sure that she felt the same way.

When he was twenty-eight, Bill was appointed to his own parish, in a venerable town on the edge of the potteries. The church was eighteenth century, substantial. Given the size of the parish, the congregation was not numerous, but it was able to muster a steady 160 on the days when a head count was deemed necessary. (It was perhaps significant that this was the number he inherited from his aged predecessor and this remained the number during the whole of his ministry there.) The large Victorian vicarage had been considered impossible to run in the late fifties and a smaller, box-like house but with a large garden was purchased by the diocese. This was their home for sixteen years. Home: a word that conjured so much, like conflict, hatred. . . . It was no wonder that both his wife and his home were relegated to the back of his mind, they caused him only angst. And he was supposed to be walking the Camino to be working through these emotions, which, apparently were only being exacerbated by his so-called companions.

There had certainly not been much mental refreshment so far on the Camino. 'But I've been doing the job everyone wanted me to do,' he said out loud. 'How would it have been if I had insisted on walking on my own in silent contemplation of my own needs?' A tiny idea intruded. Maybe that was the whole point of a pilgrimage, though? Then, introspection was all very well. It prevented you from seeing every sign along the pilgrim route. Someone had to make sure they did not get lost.

The comradeship between Rebecca and Oliver lasted for less than half an hour. They had been discussing birds, disagreeing as to whether what they were seeing was a vulture or an eagle of some sort. Oliver remarked innocently that he most enjoyed walking with Ella. 'She's very knowledgeable about all sorts of things.'

Unaccountably stung by what she took to be implied criticism of her lack of knowledge, Rebecca retorted, 'I'm so sorry she's not with you instead of me. As you say, I'm sure Ella would have the answer for you and with a bit of luck she'll be back with us soon and you can spend all your spare time looking after her.'

'That sounded unnecessarily nasty.'

And he was right, thought Rebecca, who could not think why she'd said it in the first place. 'I was talking about my deficient wildlife education,' she replied flatly.

'I don't understand you,' he retorted. 'You've already admitted you know Ella. You told me so when we met in Harrods. I should have thought you'd be glad to have a friend along. Or is it that you are afraid she'll tell us all about something in your past you'd rather remain hidden?'

Rebecca looked at him scathingly. 'You are ridiculous,' she commented and turned away.

'All right. I apologize. But you know, you always give the impression of wishing Ella were anywhere but on this pilgrimage.' He said shrewdly, 'I think you may have forgotten no one actually chooses to permit Ella to do things. That is a very independent lady. Or hadn't you noticed?'

He was too perspective by half. Rebecca snapped, 'What I observe is that you and I have so little to say to each other that doesn't degenerate into a rotten row we are best apart, so I'll drop back and let you contemplate the scenery on your own since you so obviously dislike my company.'

'On the contrary, since you seem so full of vigour I suggest you lead the way for a change. I'm going to have a pee,' and he got up from the rock on which they were sitting and walked away from her.

Routed, Rebecca strode ahead.

And so it was in a long, straggly uncommunicative line that they reached the centre of Santo Domingo de la Calzada, half of them abashed by their behaviour, yet unrepentant.

Jonah, who had sauntered at the rear seemingly oblivious of the tensions ahead, found himself a bed in the old pilgrim refuge. The others walked on to the recently restored parador – one of the most resplendent of the paradors on the Camino, a former twelfth-century hospital built on the remains of a palace belonging to the monarchs of Navarre, its thick stone pillars supporting a vaulted ceiling, with deep leather chairs in the foyer. And there waiting for them, they discovered Ella.

'You look so much better,' exclaimed Oliver, hugging her.

'Thank you, I am much restored.'

'How long are you staying?' asked Bill politely.

'For as long as you are. Then I'll walk a couple of days with you.'

'That's great,' said Oliver, sounding so sincere that both Bill and Rebecca felt thoroughly ashamed of their less than enthusiastic welcome.

'Then we'll catch up with the news at dinner,' said Rebecca.

By dinner time frayed tempers had been restored. Perhaps it

was the hills, or the silence, or both, or even their present surroundings, but all were disposed to be polite to each other and both Bill and Philip had decided not to make their usual snide comments about Jonah.

'I have a treat in store for you,' Jonah announced, having arrived from the refuge, as they sat down together in the dining room. 'Or do you all know that a live cock and hen live inside the church?'

'You're joking.'

Rebecca, at least, could be relied on not to have read the legends, and Jonah grinned at her. 'It was in the middle ages, you see. A man and his wife and son came on pilgrimage and when they got to Santo Domingo the innkeeper's daughter fell for the son who was called Hugonell. But Hugonell spurned her and to punish him she hid a silver goblet in his luggage.'

'Very Joseph and the Amazing Technicolor Waistcoat,' said Ella.

'Dreamcoat,' corrected Philip.

'Just so. Obviously it was found, he was arrested and hanged for a thief.'

'Tough.'

'Very. The parents were distraught, but they distinctly heard Hugonell telling them that he wasn't dead because St Dominic was holding him up by the feet. Of course they went immediately to the judge to tell him the good news.'

'Naturally.'

'But the judge refused to believe them. He was dining. In front of him was a platter on which was a pair of roast chickens. He said that if the boy were alive St Dominic could prove it by restoring life to the chickens. . . .'

'Which got up and flew away.'

'You have heard the story before.'

'No, but it seemed obvious,' Rebecca smiled. 'So the boy was innocent and lived? Good story.'

'If they crow tomorrow when you see them, it's good luck.'

'Poppycock,' said Bill, and Ella choked and had to be thumped on the back by Oliver.

Ella had known immediately they entered the bar where they

were forgathering that Oliver and Rebecca had had another disagreement. When tackled by her, Oliver insisted that it was really only a minor row, but Ella did so hope it wasn't over herself (she was not so naïve as to discount that very possibility).

So perhaps it was the men's determination not to rock a boat that had suddenly become unstable, or the women's to follow their example – or maybe just the prospect of a free day to come – but they drank more than usual.

Philip and Ella were the first to leave the table; Ella because to her suddenly the gaiety seemed forced, Philip because his bladder was too full for comfort. At any rate, they disappeared together towards the lifts, leaving, as it happened, Bill and Rebecca to follow them.

They were in the lift. As the doors closed Bill said, in a disparaging tone, 'I do wonder at parents who bring small children to a place like this. It's so disruptive to the other guests.'

'I beg your pardon?'

'Those two children in the foyer. You must have seen them. A boy and a girl aged about six and eight. So unsuitable.'

'I didn't see. . . .' Toby? Charley? How could she have missed them? They must have been waiting for her to come out of the dining-room. In total panic Rebecca pressed every button on the panel. Nothing happened. 'Let me out. Let me see them. Do something,' she shrieked, pounding on the lift doors.

'Rebecca. What in heaven's name is the matter?'

The lift stopped with a jerk and she was thrown against Bill. Instinctively he put his arms round her, though there was no manner of comfort in his touch for his body was stiff with rejection. She was panting, like a wild thing. 'You shouldn't travel in lifts if you suffer from claustrophobia,' he said, reaching the only logical conclusion, that Rebecca was hysterical because of a fear of enclosed spaces.

'You stupid man. . . .' Rebecca slumped against him, the tears streaming down her face. 'You know nothing about it. Nothing.'

Her weeping was profound. It seemed that the well from which her tears flowed was bottomless. It was a thing totally beyond Bill's experience, his own wife maintaining a placid exterior under all circumstances. (Incongruously, he was struck by the notion that Mary's temperament could not have been all that placid, after all.) There seemed nothing for it but to stay where he was, with Rebecca in his arms, until she had recovered. And then the doors opened.

Facing them was Oliver. What was he to think? That Bill had taken some sort of advantage of the weeping woman; that she was deeply upset by something he had done?

After a moment Rebecca sensed that the doors had opened. She moved and Bill's arms, defiantly still where they were, dropped from her shoulders. Rebecca, her eyes still streaming with tears, turned away, pushing past Oliver without a word.

'It's not how it looks,' Bill said quietly.

'How does it look?'

'That I was taking advantage of her. For some reason she just became hysterical.'

'She certainly seemed upset.'

'Upset.' Bill shook his head. 'I knew it was going to end like this. First we have an old woman who can't maintain the pace. Then we have an unstable one to cope with. I knew all along it was a risk bringing women on the Camino.'

Somehow Oliver was inclined to believe Bill about not taking advantage of Rebecca. It seemed unlikely, for both of them. The other was too much. 'How can you be so sexist? So Ella got tired. So what? As for Rebecca, you must have done something, said something. What on earth was it?'

Bill heaved an aggrieved sigh. 'We got into the lift together. That's all.'

'You must have done something, said something.'

'I was merely commenting on the unsuitability of this place for small children when she suddenly went berserk. Don't ask me how, or why.'

'You were talking about children?'

'Not talking about them. I just said—'

'So you told me.' Children. Having them. Not having them. Not wanting Ella to walk with them. Because Ella knew something about Rebecca that they did not?

'Do you have children, Bill?' Oliver asked conversationally as they walked down the corridor together. He had the idea it might be as well to deflect the man's mind from the Rebecca thing.

'My wife and I were blessed with only one child,' said Bill formally. 'A daughter,' he added.

'You'd not mentioned your wife before.'

'There was no need to.' He paused. 'We are separated,' Bill admitted reluctantly.

'I'm sorry.'

'Why should you be? She is worthless. The only thing to be sorry about is the time I took to find that out.'

There was no answer to that, but the corridor was long. 'You must still miss your daughter.'

Bill shrugged. 'When you are married, you may know differently.' He stopped beside his door. 'In the meantime I should be grateful if you would not mention any of this.'

'As you wish. Good night.'

They had called her Elspeth. Bill and Elspeth had a love-hate relationship from her fifth birthday when, realizing that they were unlikely to have more children and recognizing finally that she was already wilful, Bill declared that their daughter must be disciplined lest she be spoilt. This declaration inevitably led to tantrums – the two were actually very much alike – which not only persisted but grew in their ferocity as the years went by. There were times when father and daughter were barely able to be civil to each other and when she was eleven Elspeth opted for a boarding school in Malvern, to which request her parents acceded thankfully and where, incidentally, she was very happy. Did he miss her? In a funny way he missed the stimulation of their arguments, the way she was so sure he was wrong, always. The way he knew he was right and that it was his God-given right to prove it to her. He'd not thought of Elspeth in weeks. He thought he might send her a postcard. And also he might try to think of a way to remove the unsuitable Rebecca from their group.

In the morning Oliver did the town with determination, bought a postcard, wrote it and posted it at the post office. His mother liked official views – everyone knew they were usually better than an amateur's photograph – so to save carrying them, he sent a card to her from each place of interest. He knew without asking that she would save them for him and as he was not carrying a camera some of them he might even beg for a keepsake. He had seen the cock and hen – and had definitely heard some sort of a croak from the cock which he took to mean that his luck would hold. He had admired the plaques commending Santo Domingo who, he discovered with a flicker of interest, was the patron saint of engineers. Now he was sitting in the square with nothing to do but to think about the event of the night before.

No. He refused to believe that Rebecca had seduced Bill into making a pass. It was equally unlikely that Bill had made a move on her. That remark about his wife was chilling. So what was it, what had so upset Rebecca? He thought it might be interesting to find out.

And in the meantime, he was becoming hungry.

# Chapter Eleven

Rebecca could not remember when she had wept quite like that. On many occasions she had felt like howling (though not at the funeral; then she was just frozen). Sometimes lumps had formed in her throat when something unexpected reminded her of something one of the children had done, something one of them had said, but inevitably she had swallowed the lumps, wiped away the unshed tears and, she now realized, all this long time she had suppressed many of the emotions the deaths of her children evoked – even while she was having treatment. That episode in the lift was exceptional. Afterwards, as she sat in her room huddled on a chair, clutching her locket in both hands, the tears would not cease, flooding down her face in an unstoppable stream and she shook like one demented. Eventually, in the small hours she became calmer, found she could move, though it was with the gait of an old woman, the shaking became an occasional shudder and her cheeks dried, stiff with salt. Mechanically she undressed, splashed cold water on her face, cleaned her teeth, lay down on the bed under a sheet and closed her swollen eyelids. She slept for twelve solid hours.

When she woke, Rebecca felt totally different. It was true that she was drained but for the first time since the death of her children she felt totally calm, resigned even. It would not last, of that she was also aware, but it was a beginning of acceptance. Rebecca was also indifferent to the witnesses to her breakdown. It was perhaps unfortunate that of all her companions she had wept in Bill's arms – such a basically unsympathetic man – but there it was. She would rest, walk the next day, and the next.

She would finish the Camino and then. . . ? It no longer seemed to matter. Something in the manner of Mr Micawber would turn up.

Some might consider it justice that of the three only Bill had a bad night. Emotions chilled him, but for some reason the feel of Rebecca in his arms in the lift as she wept on his shoulder triggered thoughts he would have given anything to forget. He tossed and turned, alternately too hot, too cold, the sheets a tangle of discomfort, his mind a turmoil, a jumble of images, words, seething anger against a biased world and Mary in particular. He, a totally innocent party to be so confounded by his own wife.

Damn woman . . . how dare she . . . betrayer of the marriage bed . . . insatiable sexual appetite. . . . The phrases rang in his brain, a musical counterpoint with an infernal rhythm like something from a devilish carousel. He would doze, to jerk awake time after time and the thing would begin again. How dare she. . . .

After the first few months of marriage when sex had been an enjoyable novelty to them both, Bill and Mary had settled into a habit of regularity. Anything but easy with spontaneity in bed, Bill was certainly happier that way. It had not once occurred to Bill to inquire if his wife felt the same. She had never complained, certainly not after Elspeth was born. There was a moment of revelation on this night as Bill contemplated for maybe five minutes the uncomfortable thought that perhaps Mary had felt differently. That perhaps there had been reason behind her betrayal. But what did she have to complain about? There had never been an instance when he had been anything less than totally faithful to her. She had everything she needed, a home, a family. A life of her own? How ridiculous. Any woman married to a man of God knew that her life would be dedicated to the service of her husband's vocation and Mary knew all about that from her own family. It was not even as though she had come to it with an enhanced view of her own place in the scheme of things. (Bill was not even ambivalent about women-clergy. He disapproved.)

It only went to prove that all women were damnably unstable, if not damned – Mary, Ella, Rebecca. Bill experienced a surge of fellow feeling towards the medieval scholars who saw women as intrinsically evil, a scourge to entrap the unwary male. Sometimes he felt that he really did not much like women. Towards dawn his broken sleep became merely uneasy and he drifted into a nightmare in which he was leading a group of cloaked pilgrims along the Camino. For some reason that eluded him they were all women. They depended on him, of course, but gradually they became wayward; they ceased to heed his advice. One day there was a storm. The fierce wind blew the women's cloaks open and he saw plainly what had been concealed from him before, that not only were the women naked, they had forked tails and cloven feet.

He woke sweating heavily, showered, dressed and fled into the church.

Unaware that he had yet to break his fast, Bill spent the morning on his knees in a corner of a side chapel reserved for the faithful. The heavy symbolism of his nightmare taunted him. Did he really think of women as devils incarnate? It was a bit over the top if he did. (Not to say very politically incorrect in this day and age.) And if he did, with what justification? Bill thought about the women he had known, really known as opposed to their being mere acquaintances. There were not many, if you discounted family: a childhood sweetheart who had gone to another school when she was nine, a theological student who had chosen the life of a missionary in Africa, a lay reader who became a nun, Mary his wife. There was no one with whom he had formed a serious relationship. He thought again about the women on the pilgrimage whose proximity he often regarded as a nuisance: Ella, whose age surely safeguarded her from being a sexual image; Rebecca, whom, if he thought of her at all, it was as an irritant (like Elspeth). As he had concluded in the night, Bill decided again that he did not much like women.

But that was no problem. It was possible that Rebecca was suffering from an unrelated misfortune – even a physical illness, he conceded. There was even the uncomfortable notion (if politically correct one) that much of the ills afflicting women were male-generated. So if he did not much care for women, did he prefer men – as friends, probably; as more than friends? At that abrupt and startling thought, Bill raised his eyes to the tortured body of the Christ that hung high on the altar before him. The implications were far beyond anything life had thrown at him so far. He thought of all the things he had said and done in the past and his soul squirmed.

And this time the sweat that broke out on Bill's body was cold.

At lunch time Philip phoned Posy. 'How was Florence?'

'Magical, especially the Uffizzi.'

'Not the shops?' There was a short pause. 'Posy?'

'We did some window shopping, yes. I bought some silver bracelets for the girls in the market.'

'Nothing for yourself? How restrained. What about the boys?'

'You know what boys are like. In the end I bought some posters. I think they'll approve of them.' Posy adored her grandchildren, as Philip was well aware.

'Have you seen much of them since you got back?'

'Enough,' she suppressed a small sigh, which nevertheless he heard. What Posy did not appreciate – and what Philip was coming slowly to understand – was the frequency with which her two daughters-in-law rang her up and asked her to babysit, for they all lived within five miles of the parental home. Worse still, they descended on her with a carful of children and assumed that not only was she ravished to see them, it was the joy of her life to feed and amuse the children (and, if necessary, put them to bed) until such time as one of their parents could come and collect them. If asked, Posy would readily have admitted that she liked nothing better than to bake the children the delicious things their mothers were too preoccupied to cook, play board games and, of course, lose. But it was not always convenient to drop everything to look after the children. 'You know, I have this sneaking suspicion that the services asked of me will become more onerous as time goes by. I seem to be expected to rally round as if I'm making up for lost time.'

'Mm,' he answered inadequately. Coping with the extended family had never impinged on his own life too badly, so far.

'I also bought silk scarves for Fiona and Gail, and silk ties for Rob and James.'

'Nothing for Matt and Eve?'

'Not at the moment. Um – how much longer is this journey going to take?'

'It's difficult to say, really. About a month, I should think,' he said cautiously. 'Why do you ask?'

'I thought I might visit Matt.'

'At sea?'

'Don't be silly, dear. Actually he phoned last night. They've arrived in Antigua. I thought I might fly out and see them for a few days.'

'Seems a long way to go for a few days.'

'I wouldn't want to push my luck with Eve. The only thing is, if I wait until you come home, would you come with me?'

'I don't think I'd want to go away for a bit after this.'

'That's what I thought. So I'll go ahead and book a flight, then?'

It was probably safer than letting her loose on the housing market. 'I thought you were house hunting?' he temporized.

'I've done that. But what I've concluded will definitely have to wait until you are home, won't it?'

That, at least, was a relief. 'I think we might find we agree about all sorts of things then,' he replied guardedly.

'Philip, you haven't said yet, how is it all going?'

'Fine. Fine.' Impossible to tell her, in under several hours. 'You'll have to read my diary when I'm home.'

'Goodness me,' she chuckled down the line. 'Nothing libellous in it?'

Philip grinned. 'Well, maybe I'll just read you the best bits. By the way, I still have that funny feeling about Bill.'

'As in funny-peculiar, I assume, not funny ha-ha?'

'You don't remember reading anything about him, do you?'

'I can't say I've given him a thought. But since you ask, I'll see what I can dredge up from the back of my mind.'

'And in the meantime, give my love to everyone.'

'Talk to you soon.'

It was late afternoon before Rebecca emerged from the parador, intending to buy a snack and to find somewhere to replace the sunglasses she had somehow lost. She rarely wore sunglasses while walking, preferring to reduce the glare with a baseball cap. But she distinctly remembered that she had put sunglasses on while she and Oliver were discussing birds. Before they had yet another of their rows. She supposed she had dropped them when she stormed off ahead of him. It was all his fault. Passivity and resignation temporarily set aside, Rebecca seethed. Oliver was an arrogant prig, suggesting that she had so little care for Ella she wished the woman were not with them. How dared he. Looking blindly into a shop window, Rebecca conceded that originally she had thought just that about Ella. Of course, it was not only Ella's age. It had taken Rebecca less than a day to realize the other woman might be a good few years older, but she was more than capable of walking the distance. Oliver had made a more than shrewd guess that Ella knew things about herself that Rebecca wished concealed. But the accusation that she cared nothing for the older woman was unfair.

Sunglasses were difficult to obtain. Eventually Rebecca found an optician who sold them – thank the lord for plastic – then Rebecca visited the cock and hen. It was a funny thing about Oliver, she thought to herself as she viewed with distaste the animals in their small cage which remained stubbornly mute. There were things about Oliver that thoroughly riled her. No matter that they started a conversation perfectly innocuously, something he said inevitably triggered a reaction in her that was nothing short of violent. Like the previous day. She was on the point of being very rude to him when he got up and left her and if he had not there was no saying what she would have done.

Rebecca sat down to consider this. She knew very well that some people are destined never to like each other. Incompatibility was a strange thing. You might be very different from someone yet have a soft spot for that person. You might also have quite a lot in common but not be able to stand each other. Now Oliver had a manner of looking at her that implied he was superior in every way. Without any justification whatsoever. Why, they had hardly spoken more than two words together about their past, how they felt about things, where they were going when the pilgrimage was over. So how would he know if he were superior or not? She had known instinctively from the first that she and Oliver were incompatible. Which was a pity, because actually they did have quite a lot in common. They were both good walkers; they both liked the quiet of the outdoors – not that they had ever discussed this, but it was quite plain to her that this was so. She suspected that Oliver, like herself, was at a decisive moment in his life. Which might have made him an obvious sounding-board for her own problems if they had not struck sparks off each other with monotonous regularity. It was all rather a shame, but she had definitely come to the conclusion the only thing to do was to stay away from him as far as possible until the end of the walk.

Having come to that decision, Rebecca resumed her study of the church. She was not sure about Spanish baroque. It was all so very over the top. She could quite believe that if you were an ordinary inhabitant of a town like this, enduring the hard life of the seventeenth century – yet with the gold of the New World behind you and with your home-grown saint – you might consider the whole thing a good investment in the afterlife. Rebecca noticed Bill on his knees in the side chapel, and wondered about that, too.

She found her way into the square and sat down. Thinking of Bill, her mind returned to the subject of incompatibility. There was no doubt that she and Bill were poles apart. He never spoke about his marital status. Somehow Rebecca had a feeling he might be divorced. And fairly recently. There was something about him that suggested Bill was used to being looked after by a woman, though she sensed about Bill an unease with females – even more after last night for there had been absolutely no solace for her in his arms. It was not that he did not care for any of them as people, just that they did not really come into his scheme of things. Anyway, you could certainly say she and Bill were incompatible, yet there was little if none of the antagonism she felt towards Oliver.

Now she actively disliked Oliver. When she was with him she wanted to boil over with frustration. She had an equable temperament, for heaven's sake. She never rowed with her work colleagues. Over the years she'd had good friends with whom she would not have dreamt of quarrelling; even the break-up with Mike had not been accompanied by any of the blazing rows she knew some divorcing couples went through, yet every time she spent more than a few minutes in Oliver's company he made her erupt. It was all so stupid. Totally ludicrous. Which meant the sensible thing to do was to stay away from him.

'You all right?'

The interruption was both intrusive and welcome. Rebecca stiffened instinctively as she looked up into Jonah's face. 'Of course I'm all right,' she answered sharply. 'Why ever would you think otherwise?'

'You look a bit drained and it wasn't that late a night.'

For a split second Rebecca was tempted to tell Jonah exactly what had happened – not only what had transpired the previous evening but all the appalling things that she had gone through recently. 'I-I. . . .'

'Yes?' he said encouragingly.

It was not possible. She could not confide in a mere boy. Rebecca shrugged. 'Just one of those things,' she said vaguely. 'I've got a bit of a headache.' Jonah looked sceptical. 'Anyway, what are you doing wandering round? You usually have an itinerary mapped out on our rest days. Becoming idle like the rest of us?' Her tone was light, mocking. It was Jonah's turn to appear defensive. Rebecca said, 'It must seem odd at times, walking with a lot of wrinklies like us. Why do you do it?'

'I told you, I like the way you operate together. Anyway, wrinklies is pejorative, innit?'

Rebecca laughed out loud. 'If you say so,' she agreed. 'Seriously, though, what do your parents think of this set-up?' There was no reply. She turned her head to look at him. 'No. I don't believe you could come on a trip like this without telling them.'

'Lot you know about it.'

'Don't they know?'

He shrugged. 'Why should they? They're dead.'

She paled. This was the other side of the coin, a boy without parents, herself without children. Was this why she had always felt something of an affinity towards Jonah?

'Rebecca? You all right?' He touched her arm. 'Not goin' to be sick are you?'

'Sorry. I-I didn't realize. You have no family? You must have someone to worry about you. Surely?'

'Only an uncle,' he said reluctantly. 'He's a good man. We keep in touch. Don't worry. I manage fine.'

'Oh.' You'd have thought an adult would have known how to cope after a bereavement. It seemed Jonah knew more about the aspects of life that mattered than she did. She was so thankful she had not poured out all her woes to him.

'You're paler than ever. Had anything to eat? I thought not. Come and have a snack with me.'

They had a snack and with it a glass of red wine, and it was afterwards that Rebecca realized that Jonah had paid for it. After that they parted and she felt sufficiently limp to indulge in a siesta. But sleep would not come immediately. How far had they come? A long way, in both terms of fellowship and mileage. Almost two weeks it had taken them to walk the 222.7 kilometres (Bill kept a daily count). At this rate it would take more than the five weeks she had allowed herself to reach Santiago. Fortunately money was not likely to be too much of a problem for she was well within her budget. But what happened then?

There was a time after the divorce when Rebecca had dreams of running a restaurant of her own. After the fire she could think of nothing further ahead than the next day. Now, suddenly, the dream was worming its way back into her consciousness. She had her share of the house money, too. Rebecca sighed. Foolish dream. The prospect of finding either the resort that appealed to her – for she had decided for the children's sake that it would not be in London – let alone the restaurant to invest in seemed more and more unlikely, though Cornwall had always seemed a good place to start looking.

Why was she surprised that her mind had become a mire of indecision, doubt and uncertainty. So much had happened to her. She had lost so much in such a short time: husband, mother, children. There was nothing left. She had a good mind to throw everything away and go abroad for a year, do the things the young were doing when she was working her guts out. Go to New Zealand.

Rebecca sat up with a jerk, sleep forgotten. So why not? Why should she not abandon everything? Surely that was wimpish. She'd always wanted her own business. Did it have to be in this country? She'd always had a hankering to see New Zealand. (Australia seemed too brash from what she'd read.) There were places in the South Island, she'd heard, where the tourists came all year round.

What were her options? What chains bound her now that nothing was left except two graves? You could not carry graves with you but the memories would always be there, wherever you went. Rebecca went cold. This was getting scary. This was in no way something you did in a hurry. Though why not?

# Chapter Twelve

So what with one thing and another it was an uneasy band that heaved backpacks on to shoulders and set off the following morning passing eventually through the Montes de Orca, steep, wild and traditionally bandit country, though they saw only two cyclists who overtook them.

Ella walked for another morning and then decided she'd make arrangements to go ahead and wait for them all in Burgos. 'So long as you promise to ring me each evening and tell me how you are.'

'Of course we will,' promised Jonah.

Between San Juan de Ortega and Burgos there were three routes, one of which was the modern track running beside a busy road and which they decided against unanimously, choosing the longer, scenic one which took them up into the Sierra de Atapuerca. The going was hard, but not so difficult that Oliver, once more in the lead by a considerable distance, was not able to let his mind wander freely. As he had said to Rebecca, he enjoyed walking with Ella, but he realized that on the days when she chose not to walk he felt free to stride out, above all, not to have to make the walk a social occasion. Somewhat to his surprise, during the morning he actually found himself missing the silent companionship of another walker behind him – all right, the companionship of Rebecca before, that is, they had had that last row. Since that afternoon, he had put it to the back of his mind, so ridiculous it had been and coming from nowhere. She was a strange girl, no mistake about it and one he could not fathom at all. And there was that equally weird episode with Bill in the lift. Well, that was the red hair for you, and he grinned to himself. Actually it was gorgeous hair, if you liked that particular colour of russet, maybe copper beech leaves when they had fallen on the forest floor and were damp with the autumn frosts. It was an odd thing how a volatile temperament went with the hair. They always said it did – and he did not bother to define the article. Which, naturally, was why, preferring the quiet life, or at least preferring women who did not make waves, he had always gone out of his way to avoid women with red hair. And would do so until the walk ended. But it was a pity, because he thought they probably had quite a lot in common. Rebecca was a good walker and she obviously liked the quiet of the outdoors. Not that he had asked her, but it was obvious when you thought about it. He had the idea that she was at a crossroads of some sort. He knew she had given up her job for he had heard her talking about it to Philip. So she was probably using this time to decide what she should do next. He wished her luck of her reflections, he thought a little grimly.

Reflections were getting him precisely nowhere. Strange that, for he had expected to have so much time to think weighty, philosophical thoughts on the pilgrimage, not to mention working out just where he was going with his life now that he had a sort-of second chance at it, but the Camino had not turned out like that at all. Much of the time was taken up with desultory, meaningless conversation with people he would never want to see again, once they had reached Santiago. Bill, for one. And Rebecca for another. His foot slipped sideways into a rut as he stumbled and the thought turned into a question that he was not able to answer immediately. Oliver righted himself. Well, of course he would not exactly go out of his way not to see anyone. . . .

So, what was he going to do once they had reached their goal? What was his goal in life now, without a worthwhile occupation yet sufficiently cushioned by money for it not to matter? Use what he had to make more? He had an idea that could be boring in the extreme, but if he did, how and where and what for? What was the point? To do good? If you meant just giving to charity, that was easy. There was nothing to stop him from doing that now. Maybe having a family, bringing up a family to good purpose was what best defined a man of the twenty-first century. If he dared take the chance that his tumour would not return. But to acquire a family a man obviously needed a wife – remembering his own childhood, Oliver was a firm believer in the desirability of two parents. So, a red-headed wife? Oliver chuckled out loud. Not on your life. But he did wonder if he had been just a little hard on her, Rebecca, that is. He really should not have said that about her not wanting Ella on the pilgrimage.

Unless there was something else bothering her. He stopped to drink some water – Bill's rigorous hourly break had long since been abandoned and they took water/comfort stops as and when they were needed. The morning's leader usually decided where to stop for lunch and they regrouped then. It seemed no surprise to him to find Rebecca pacing him, if far enough back for him not to have been aware of her.

'Hi,' he said.

'Hi, yourself.' They drank in silence.

Oliver hefted his backpack into a comfortable position. 'You coming with me, or do you want to walk on your own?'

Rebecca shook her head. It was oddly comforting to be with another person. She had had altogether too much time for reflection – brooding. 'But we don't have to talk, if you'd rather not,' she added hastily.

They walked on in silence, Oliver in the lead since the path was too narrow to walk abreast. It was still a companionable silence, though it did not last.

'Rebecca? Look, I know it's probably. . . .'

'None of my business?' she supplied.

Oliver stopped. To his relief Rebecca was smiling. 'No. But – but that evening in the lift when. . . .'

'When you found me in floods of tears?'

'When I found you in Bill's arms. Was he – I mean, had he. . . .'

'Molested me? Good heavens, what do you take me for?'

'Seriously, there must have been some reason. Do you want – need to tell anyone about it?'

'It's not what you think.' Rebecca sighed. She supposed she'd always known it would become common knowledge. Jonah had almost been the recipient of her sorrows. She'd never thought it would be Oliver whom she told first. Except for Ella who already knew. 'My children died in a fire. Nearly ten months ago. Bill said he'd seen two children in the foyer. I thought . . . I thought. . . . Actually, I suppose I threw a wobbly.' You had to give Ella credit for her discretion. In all that time she obviously hadn't told either Oliver, or Bill. Not by the way Oliver was reacting now. 'Bill, of course, thinks I'm an unstable fool who suffers from claustrophobia.'

'He'd seen your dead children?'

She grimaced. 'What do you think? Of course he hadn't. And I wasn't even aware that there were children in the foyer. But yes, I believed Bill had seen something I was meant to see. I went a bit crazy. Put like that, of course, I sound an absolute nutter. I bet Bill thinks so.'

'You haven't told Bill what really happened?'

'Would you?'

Of course he would not. 'Ella knows?'

'She lives next door to my mother. To where my mother lived before she died,' Rebecca corrected herself. She sighed again. 'Sorry, Oliver. You did ask. You might as well hear it all.' She told him the whole story – baldly. It did not take so very long – not even doing something she had never envisaged, for Rebecca undid the second button of her shirt, drew out the locket hidden there and opened it to show Oliver the faces of her children.

He was very moved. To her surprise, when she had finished he said nothing but took her into his arms and just held her. It was so different from the way Bill had held her in the lift. Then it was as if he were holding her in check. This was consolation.

It was a morning of surprises. It felt right. She was tall enough to fit comfortably so that the top of her head rested under his chin. Oliver made no attempt to say anything. If she had not been wearing her backpack he might have stroked her. He did nothing.

Which was just the right reaction. After a while Rebecca moved.

'You must have gone through hell.'

'I am going through hell.'

'I'm sorry if I've made things more difficult.'

'You haven't.' She meant it. She realized that in a bizarre way the tension between them had prevented her from agonizing quite as much as she might otherwise have done. She told him so.

'I'm glad. Not about the rows,' he said humbly. 'About the other thing. Rebecca, do you mind if the others get to hear about – about what happened?'

'I'd rather they didn't. I don't want anyone's pity. No, I suppose I've always known they would find out, sooner or later.'

'Come on, we ought to be looking for a place for lunch.' They walked on, side by side now and, unaccountably, Rebecca felt as though a chink had appeared in the dark curtain that had obliterated her light for aeons.

They reached a fork in the road. Oliver stopped. 'Which way?' he asked.

'I don't know. Where's our marker shell?' The scallop shell was the Camino's way mark and painted or sculpted shells were to be found somewhere at every fork on the route.

'There's nothing on any of these stones.' A partly collapsed wall made up both forks of the junction.

'I don't see anything on the path ahead, or on a tree.'

'There's also been no one in sight for ages.'

'Then we'll just have to wait while the rest catch us up. They're probably less than five minutes behind.'

They sat down to wait, sharing a bar of chocolate. After ten minutes, a small concern seeped into Oliver's mind. He'd not consciously registered a marker shell for some kilometres. Since after Rebecca had joined him. Was it possible that he could have taken a wrong turning? After twenty minutes there seemed no doubt about it. 'Oh, damn,' he said resignedly. 'Who said there was always some idiot who took the wrong turning?'

Rebecca smiled. (She'd noticed recently that her face was becoming far more flexible, that smiles came more readily.) 'Did we go wrong before, or after I joined you, do you think?'

'Probably after. I expect it was my fault.' He took out the map he always carried and attempted to work out where they were. 'Look, I think we must be here. It seems safest to keep walking west – until we see someone to ask.'

That did not happen for almost an hour. Then on the outskirts of an apparently deserted village they came upon another fork in the road, where an old woman was tending a small garden behind the wall. In halting Spanish Oliver asked where they were. She did not understand.

'Burgos?' Rebecca said. 'The Camino?'

The reply came immediately, excitedly, as the woman pointed away from the direction Oliver would have pursued. He shrugged, but they thanked her and walked away. There was a croaking call and behind him the sound of shuffling feet. They both turned and amidst a flow of almost incomprehensible Spanish she thrust several shrivelled apples into his hand.

'Nice of her, but what was that all about?'

'A phrase I think I understand: *Pilgrim, pray for me*.' And once again there were tears in Rebecca's eyes which she did not attempt to conceal.

'Rebecca. Are you all right,' he asked anxiously.

'As if my prayers could help anyone.'

'I'm sure they'd wing their way faster than most. Come here. I'd give you a hug, if I could get my arms round that backpack.' He took hold of her hand and patted it instead. 'Take it as read.'

They trudged on, hoping against hope to come upon their companions before too long – or at least find a hint that they had gone ahead. There was another fork, this one shaded by a giant oak, under it a large flat-topped rock. Sitting on the rock in the shade of the giant oak was the dark-clad, brooding figure of a man, his drooping head supported on one hand, pilgrim staff in the other.

Oliver's quick gasp of awe was involuntary and in the same instant as Rebecca's muttered, 'Good heavens, Santiago.'

'There you are,' said Jonah, stretching as he rose from the rock. 'What kept you so long?'

'You came to find us?' asked Rebecca.

'Nah. Just thought I'd wait where you was bound to turn up.'

'Thanks, all the same,' said Oliver.

They went on together. 'Here,' said Oliver, surprised to feel so touched that it was Jonah who had realized what had happened. 'Have an apple.' He hesitated. 'I didn't nick it. If you don't mind the whimsy, I think it's been blessed.'

Rebecca told him about the old woman. 'They may look shrivelled. They're very sweet.'

'Bound to be blessed,' agreed Jonah. 'They take the Camino seriously in these parts.'

In the distance the group was sitting on the ground under a tree having lunch. The three slowed to a stroll, admitted only to a small diversion.

After lunch Oliver deliberately waited for Rebecca and began to walk beside her.

'I thought you'd prefer to be in the lead again this afternoon,' she said.

'I guess I did enough of that this morning. I'm sorry I led you astray.'

She smiled – and this time it was almost a grin. 'It was as much my fault. I didn't notice a thing. And I'm all right at the back. You don't have to do penance.'

'I know that,' he answered. 'And I'm not.'

'Then why . . . I've been thinking. You were kind this morning. Kinder than I had a right to expect.'

'Right to expect?' he repeated. 'Whatever do you mean?' He sounded a little irritated.

'I irritate you. Like now. Sometimes deliberately.' She went a bit pink at the admission.

Oliver laughed. 'You have done. And I've fallen for it. Next time I'll bite my tongue before I snap back.'

She shook her head. 'I guess you don't have much faith in me.'

'It's not you, it's. . . .'

'Predictable. Red hair. Oh, Oliver.'

'Come on, if we don't get a move on Jonah will be coming back to find us again.' The morning's confession had drained her, he was aware of that at lunch time. It had not dampened her spirits, he was thinking with a sudden lift of his heart. Once more they walked together in silence, and the only thing to cross between them this time was the packet of eucalyptus sweets that Rebecca had found on her excursion to buy new sunglasses.

It was when she was unpacking at the Mesón del Cid where they were booked in for two nights that she realized the new sunglasses were missing. 'I don't believe it.' But they were. She worked out that they must have dropped out of the side pocket of her backpack when she and Oliver had stopped for a drink of water and she had first produced the eucalyptus sweets. 'Oliver's fault I didn't check. Bother him,' she said, but this time she did not sound cross at all.

# Chapter Thirteen

Burgos, capital of the kingdom of Castile, had been a cathedral city since 1075, with thirty-two hospitals in medieval times available for the use of pilgrims. The band was booked into the Mesón del Cid for two nights, a parador facing the cathedral, full of antique furniture and pilgrim artefacts – so Jonah left them there to find the municipal hostel and a bed for himself, promising to be back for dinner.

Philip limped up the stone steps to the hotel, taking off his boots in his room with a more than usually relieved grunt, dropping them on the floor with a thud. He had a nasty suspicion that he was developing yet another blister. This time it was his right heel, but even contorting over it he could not really see how big it was. He had a bath, changed, put on sandals and picked up his rudimentary first aid kit. Then he knocked on the door of the next room.

'What's the matter?' Ella asked as she opened the door to him.

'Not sure. Think I might have the beginnings of another blister. It's under my foot so I can't examine it properly. I've had a bath,' he added humbly.

'Would you like me to look at it?'

He sat down, held his foot towards her, toes pointing up. 'Just tell me if there's a blister there, under the heel.'

Ella frowned. 'Gracious me. How long have you been walking on this?'

'It was a bit sore a couple of days ago.'

'And you didn't put anything on it?'

'There didn't seem to be anything radically wrong. How big is it?' Ella traced the blister with her finger. He flinched. 'You're tickling. Put your finger on it.'

'I just did.'

'You can't have.'

She produced a small mirror. 'See for yourself.'

It was massive, fully five centimetres in diameter, covering the bottom of his heel. 'Damn,' he swore softly, awestruck.

'Does it hurt?'

'Only when I walk.'

'Silly question. Do you have blister plasters?' He produced them for her. 'Have you any idea how it happened?'

Philip shrugged. 'I thought I'd picked up a bit of grit. Told Bill I had. In fact I used it as an excuse to drop back and not to have to talk to him at all. He does go on a bit if you walk with him.'

'I wouldn't know,' said Ella. 'He doesn't walk with me. So, had you?'

'Had I what? Oh. Actually, I wriggled my foot a bit and it seemed easier, so I didn't take the boot off. Stupid.'

'It's as well we're here for a couple of nights. You'd better rest and not do too much sightseeing. Otherwise you'll be taking the bus, like me, and I'm sure you wouldn't want to do that.'

'Not because I wouldn't care for your company,' he said gallantly. 'But I would hate not to finish this with everyone because I had to drop back. And as I am beginning to suffer from mental indigestion, I'll take your advice. Thanks, Ella. I'll buy you a drink in the bar when you're ready.'

'I shall be no more than ten minutes.'

'Great. That'll give me time to phone Posy.' Philip got through straight away and told her all about his blister.

Posy was taking a flight to Antigua the next morning. She was suitably sympathetic but cut him short. 'If you've got a pen handy, I'll give you Matt's number. You can call me in a couple of days. I expect you'll be fine if you don't do too much tomorrow. Anyway, blister plasters are marvellous nowadays.'

Philip had expected more commiseration from his wife concerning his state of health. Her mild indifference disappointed him. He limped down to the bar where Ella was already describing graphically the size of his injury. The others all offered advice and showed their concern for him. 'I'm sure I'll be able to walk after a day's rest,' he reassured them, buying another round.

It was no more than he would have expected of them, he thought gratefully. Then, caring for each other was what they'd promised to do, on the Camino. (Though blisters weren't quite in the seriously ill category.)

'Red for you, Ella?'

'Thank you. I think I'm developing quite a taste for the red, especially since Rebecca said red wine is better for you. All those whatsits.'

'Flavonoids. Good for the heart. I'll join you,' said Jonah.

'How come you know a thing like that?' asked Rebecca.

'I did a stint behind the bar, didn't I.'

'Flavonoids?'

'They say they may mop up potentially harmful free radicals, or some such stuff.'

'And white wine doesn't have them?'

'So they say.'

Bill, a non-contributor, listened morosely. So it had been genuine, that excuse of Philip's. If only he had not jumped to the wrong conclusion, that the man was trying to avoid him. In a further agony of self-abasement he knew that it all went to prove what a disaster he was in general over relationships. Sometimes he wondered how he had ever got into the business of being a parish priest. In a rare fit of humility, he wondered if there had ever been a time when he had been of the slightest help to anyone over anything, let alone a matter of faith.

Jonah was saying, 'The church of Santa Gadea is where El Cid forced Alfonso VI to his knees to swear that he had no part in the death of his brother, Sancho. And did you know that in the monastery of Las Huelgas Reales there is a seated statue of St James which has actually bestowed knighthoods in the past.'

'However did it do that?'

'It has an articulated arm,' grinned Jonah. 'I'm not really the source of infallible information. I read about it in the guide book. Some of you shouldn't take me so literally.'

With guffaws of 'Cheeky brat,' 'Most of it's still nonsense,' and, 'At least you make us laugh, dear,' they moved off to the restaurant.

Making a conscious effort, Bill offered to pay for Jonah's dinner.

Over the Atlantic the next day, Posy thought about her husband with a twinge of guilt that she had been a little peremptory with him. She wondered vaguely what she'd do if Philip became ill. Not short-term. You could cope with that. She meant long-term. Like his having Alzheimer's. God, that was awful. Even thinking about it was horrendous. *Suffering it yourself*. Though a doctor school-friend once told her that the one good thing about dementia was that you didn't know you had it.

The next days were a hard slog, days during which they walked in the main stretched out in a long line, sometimes with Oliver in the lead, sometimes Bill, half-a mile back Philip, favouring his blister which, while no longer acutely painful, was a constant reminder of his human frailty. They started early but long before midday a ferocious sun that was inescapable seemed determined to extract from them every last vestige of energy. They rested for an hour or so when it was hottest, but often the shade was meagre. There was little conversation then or even when one stopped for a sip of water, a short pause and another overtook. Their backpacks seemed to weigh twice as heavily, their feet were leaden. It was as if whatever lubricated their human contact had run too thin under the unrelenting sky to permit of unnecessary expenditure of it.

In Frómista they intended staying for two nights so the refuge was barred to them and instead they found rooms in a house. Somehow that rest day was even more needed than usual – it had been hotter than ever. *Nine months of winter, three months of hell*, said the Castilian proverb. Even the September sun was blistering to northern skins. They ate their simple evening meal – cold potato omelette with slices of a fiery, wind-dried chorizo – in muted comradeship.

But Frómista was something of a gem, a small Romanesque church with an amazing interior, capitals riotously carved with biblical scenes, amongst them a sinuous snake making up to a coy Eve which had Rebecca, averse to slithery things since childhood, coming out in goose pimples and escaping into the sun. Outside, in the square was Jonah, gazing up at a statue. 'It's the Dominican friar, Pedro Gonzalez Telmo, born here in 1190,' he said, 'he became St Elmo, the patron saint of sailors.'

'However do you do a thing like that from a village such as this?' Rebecca asked.

'Frómista is very old and it was once a major halt on the Camino. Anyway, St Elmo obviously made good, and I suppose it's only fitting he should be guarding the square from the bow of a departing stone boat, blessing us as he rocks over the waves.'

Ella walked with them for the next fifty-seven kilometres to Sahagún. There, Jonah reckoned he had the best of the accommodation as the pilgrim refuge was almost sumptuous. He didn't say, but afterwards Ella thought he might have spent his second night under the stars. Sahagún was unremarkable, redeemed mainly by the brass scallop shells set in the pavements to indicate the Camino. 'Almost as though they wanted us out, fast,' grumbled Philip, 'which is fine by me.'

'I've had enough for the time being,' announced Ella. 'I'll see you all in León.'

In León the little band stepped into luxury at the Hostal San Marcos – at one time the private house of the Caballeria (Knights) of Santiago and now a restored parador – leaving Jonah to find his own bed somewhere cheaper.

Before Rebecca even unpacked that evening, she changed a £50 traveller's cheque in the hotel lobby. She put the small change into her purse which, because she intended also to look at postcards, she slipped into her pocket, and the larger notes she then put away into a pocket in her bumbag. But instead of returning to her room immediately, she walked through the main entrance to view the astonishing façade of the plateresque monastery next door in the evening sun, all statues, crosses and scallop shells.

As she was examining it, she was approached by a tall young man, with short, fair hair, a clean white T-shirt, clean blue jeans and Nike trainers. 'Señorita, would it be possible . . . you must think it very forward . . . you see, I have left my guide book in my hotel.'

It was like Mike and the smoked salmon all over again, she thought. If there was anything more calculated to make Rebecca wary it was being approached by a total stranger. She knew what he would say before his next words emerged.

'Would you be so kind as to permit me to read about Santiago Matamoros?' pointing at the statue of St James the Moor-slayer over the entrance to the monastery. His accent she thought was vaguely Scandinavian. He smiled engagingly and she felt churlish at having hesitated for a second. Maybe it was the Nike trainers that convinced her he was not one of your down-and-outs.

'Just for a moment,' she said, and held out the book to him. 'I have to go soon.'

He read swiftly. 'It is amazing, no?' Then he dismissed the whole edifice, 'If you like that sort of thing.'

Rebecca, who was inclined to agree, nevertheless began to demur, then someone brushed against her. 'Look where you're going, fool,' the young man said sharply, taking her arm as if to protect her.

The offender was another young man, shorter, dark-haired. With a sneer he turned swiftly and made a V-sign to which the first man replied in fluent Spanish, the meaning of which was perfectly plain.

It seemed altogether unnecessary. 'It's quite all right, really,' Rebecca protested. 'I'm sure it was an accident.'

The verbal exchange became heated. A fist was raised. For a shocking moment a fight seemed inevitable.

There were other people nearby, Japanese tourists, their heads studiously turned towards their group leader. Rebecca cast them a despairing glance, realizing immediately that she had to deal with this on her own. 'Just give me back my guidebook and go away, both of you,' she said tersely. The whole episode was horrible, scary. All she wanted was the safety of the

San Marcos. But it was not finished. As the young men appeared to calm down she realized almost instantly what had happened. 'My bumbag. You cut it from my waist. It's gone.' She was no fool. 'You did it. You set me up. Both of you.' Involuntarily her hands went not to her waist but to her throat – the locket was still there – but as she screamed the accusation the formerly uninvolved bystanders began to take a more obvious interest.

What happened next was outrageous. A look, of unmistakable hatred, swept across the face of the fair-haired man. Rebecca froze and when he charged at her she was incapable of moving aside. He collided with her deliberately, hitting her a glancing blow with his shoulder and she fell heavily, striking her forehead on the pavement and lapsing momentarily into unconsciousness.

Oliver had also been into the plaza. Returning to the hotel, he saw a small group of excited, gesticulating Japanese tourists clustered round a recumbent figure. Normally he would not have lingered, but something about the figure made him pause and as he did so he recognized Rebecca's red hair.

She came back to consciousness with her head cradled in Oliver's lap and his anxious face leaning over her. 'What happened? They're saying you were mugged. Are you all right?'

Was she? Rebecca blinked, moved her head warily. It throbbed. She put up a hand and discovered a large bump. 'Ouch.'

'Don't move. They're fetching someone from the hotel to check on you. Were you mugged?'

'It's all right, Oliver. I'm fine, except for where I hit my head when I fell.' She moved and her head hurt, but it was all too public and she wanted quiet and privacy. Wincing, she pushed him away. 'Come on, help me up. I feel an awful fool, lying on the pavement. Please, Oliver.'

Reluctantly, and very carefully, he helped her to her feet and with his arm firmly round her, he guided her into the foyer where they were met by a man carrying a first-aid bag who quickly ushered them both into the manager's office.

Then it became tedious. First there was a quick check-up, the bump was dabbed with antiseptic, they were urged to go to the hospital.

Rebecca said a firm, 'No.'

The tourist police arrived. She had the impression they had seen this so many times before they were only going through the motions. Her papers? Fortunately Rebecca had put her passport into a zipped pocket of her shorts – where she also kept her credit card. What had been stolen was a folder of traveller's cheques and money along with a hankie and a lipstick. The money would not be recovered. The cheques could be replaced. The explanation of it all was lengthy and involved. 'Thank God you arrived when you did,' she told Oliver, 'otherwise I'd probably be waiting in A & E only to be told what I already know – there's nothing radically wrong with me.'

There was something different about this incident, though. 'You understand, this is not the first time something like this has happened. Señora, we should like you to come to the station tomorrow and look at some photographs.'

Rebecca caught Oliver's eye. He was grinning. 'That sounds like an invitation I couldn't possibly decline.'

'Not in front of my hotel it hasn't happened before,' an irate manager snapped. 'Señora,' bowing over her, 'you have my most profound apologies.'

She inclined her head graciously and winced.

'I think you should be in bed,' said Oliver.

'Certainly not. I've only eaten bread and cheese today. And I'm starving.'

'Of course you are, señora. There will be our best table for you, and the señor, whenever you are ready. And, of course, you will be the guests of the San Marcos tonight.'

The señor, at least, appeared quite happy with the arrangements.

'So, señor. You will escort the señora to see us tomorrow?' the policeman persisted.

'Of course I shall come. But it's not necessary for you to have your day messed up, Oliver.'

'On the contrary, señora. There is a distinct possibility that the señor may have seen more than he realizes. He may well have noticed one of the gang walking away from the scene. Oh, yes. There is a gang. There are three of them. The first, in this case the fair-haired man, engages the victim in conversation, the second instigates the argument, the third steals the bag, the wallet, whatever – in your case, as you so rightly surmised, he slit the strap of your bag with a knife. I think you were wearing it loose round your waist?'

'It's more comfortable that way in the heat.'

'Undoubtedly, but in a crowd a bag worn loosely round the waist is no more safe than a shoulder bag. So, in the fracas, the actual thief walks away unnoticed. Should anyone challenge either of the other two, you'll not find a thing on them. The fair-haired man must have been most surprised you guessed what had happened. I believe that is why he knocked you down.'

'It happened to a friend of mine. In London.'

'Ah, London,' as though that explained it.

'That's why I realized what they'd done.'

'Then, until tomorrow, señora. *Buenas noches*.'

There were further apologies from the manager who seemed to be taking the whole incident personally. 'Señora, you will not forget to cancel your traveller's cheques? As soon as possible?' Then they were free to go.

'I sent a message to Ella to tell her we are delayed and for them not to wait for us,' Oliver told her. 'Meet you here in about an hour?'

'It can't be that late already,' she exclaimed, looking at her watch. It was nine o'clock.

'Time does fly when you're having fun,' he said drily. 'I'm afraid tomorrow will be just as bad. Rotten luck. Go on, go and have that bath.'

She smiled. 'I certainly need it.' She hesitated. 'Thanks, Oliver. I really don't know how I'd have handled all that without you.'

'You'd have coped.' He looked at her critically. 'You sure you're up to a meal in the restaurant? You do look a bit pale.'

'With a vast, black bruise?'

He shook his head. 'It's just a bit pink, that's all.' Then he surprised them both. He bent down and very gently put his lips to the bruise. 'Bit posh, this place. Go and put your glad rags on.'

# Chapter Fourteen

Next morning the others clustered round Bill's table. 'Rebecca's having breakfast in her room before going to the police station,' he told them. 'She doesn't seem to have suffered any ill effects, thank God.'

'You've seen her?' asked Ella.

'Oliver's spoken to her on the phone. He's going with her.'

'That's good. She'll be all right, then.'

'She'll be fine,' said Jonah, arriving just then from his hostel. 'You ready, Ella?'

'We were talking about Rebecca. I'll need to go to my room first. Poor Rebecca. What a thing to happen,' and she hurried away.

'You'll have a bit of a wait.' said Philip. 'Our rooms are at the other end of the hotel. Want some coffee?'

'Are you coming with us?' asked Jonah, declining it.

'I'll catch the stained glass tonight in the evening sun, if there is any, but I'm going to have a really lazy day. I'm finding all this baroque stuff a bit too much of a good thing.' He was going to find a quiet seat in a park, he'd decided, and write down some lines that had been going round his head for several days. He thought there might be a poem there, somewhere. It had come to him that nowadays a lot of poets didn't bother about scansion or rhyming, things that he'd been taught at school. Of course, he had an idea that you couldn't altogether abandon rules and he'd have to go into that when he got home and could look up books, but for now he just wanted to get some words down on paper. Philip was looking forward to the morning on his own. He thought he'd find a tapas bar and have a couple of glasses of wine at lunch time. That would give him time for a siesta before he ambled along to the cathedral to see the stained glass. Then, there'd be dinner. It promised to be a good day. He was glad that everyone else seemed to be occupied. It certainly let him off the hook.

Jonah and Ella duly admired the cathedral. Ella was bowled over by the stained glass. 'So much of it.'

'You need to see it with the light streaming through,' Jonah pointed out. 'Shame it's overcast.'

'I shall definitely come back this evening.'

'If you look carefully over there, you'll find a green man,' and Jonah steered her towards it.

'What's a green man?' asked Ella curiously.

'Some say the green man is a fertility symbol, or a druid, or the origin of those giants carved out of chalk downs. Others identify him as Pan, John the Baptist or Robin Hood and there's also a fascinating link in Spain to Santiago Matamoros. Who knows? Your green man's actual origins are lost in the mists of time but you'll find them all over the Celtic world, from Europe to India, wherever some stonemason with either a sense of humour or a grudge has slipped one in amongst the gargoyles. You'll know them by the foliage coming out of their mouths. There were a couple on the walls of San Martin in Frómista.'

'It's an odd interest for a young man. Whatever got you into it?'

'Well, you know. It was a family thing.' He sounded evasive.

'Fascinating.'

'And now we must touch the Puerta del Perdón.'

'What's the Puerta del Perdón?'

'It's actually just a door but you know, there have been hundreds of pilgrims who never made Santiago. They got sick. Some died. Sometime, I'm not sure when, it was decreed that those who got as far as León and touched the Puerta del Perdón would have their sins forgiven just as if they'd reached Compostela.'

Ella shuddered. 'Anything the matter?' asked Jonah.

'Nothing. Just a ghost walking over my grave. Have you told

Lover's Lane and he's never brought her home. No better than she should be, Aunt Ethel says.'

'Maybe he has two on the go.'

'Face like a frog, I heard, but probably has money. He'd not be averse to that.'

Cold with apprehension, Ella managed a weak laugh. 'Then that lets me out.'

'Trouble is,' said Winnie shrewdly, 'with that big house of your dad's a man'd not be to blame for thinking there was money there. You'll have to watch out for fortune hunters, Ella.'

There was another girl, from another village, made pregnant by Ronald in the early days of his courting of Ella. A date was set for the wedding. Shattered by this betrayal, Ella accosted Ronald in the market garden, pleading with him. How could he marry someone else when he swore he loved her?

'It ain't no use, luv. Her father's settin' us up, you know. Bought us a cottage. Because of the baby,' and to her dismay she discerned pride in his voice. 'Your father do the same if I married you? Set us up?' And when she shook her head he continued, 'Well, then. Course, I still love you, you know that. Want to meet me tonight?' and he winked and leered at her in a way she suddenly found most distasteful.

That night, in the privacy of her room she wept into her pillow and cursed, both at Ronald for his single-minded concupiscence and her own naïvety. Men, she decided at long last, both as fathers and lovers were one of life's scourges which you bore, up to a point, then put firmly in their place.

It was a fact that, though she made good friends of several men over the years, Ella never entered into another intimate relationship: she maintained, though, a certain hold over her father from that day until he died.

A satisfying life, if sometimes a lonely one, Ella concluded as she returned to the parador to change for dinner. Was this why she was so enjoying the companionship of Oliver and Jonah, the son or grandson she might have had if things had been different? Whatever, this was the only other adventure in her life and if it were to be her last, it was enough.

*

Jonah was already in the bar with Ella when Oliver and Rebecca appeared. The girl was looking tired but composed and her tan more or less concealed any mark on her forehead. 'What a day,' she exclaimed. 'I wouldn't want to go through too many of those.'

'Are you all right? Come and sit down. What are you drinking?'

'Oliver's getting me a manzanilla, thanks. You know, he's been wonderful, today.'

'Are you able to tell us what happened, or would you rather not?' asked Ella.

'I was a total fool,' the still-shaken Rebecca admitted. 'I needed to change money and thought I might just as well do it in the hotel. I must have been a bit careless and put the notes away in full view of everyone else in the foyer. It was just my luck there were thieves watching.'

'You'd have thought in a place like this a woman'd be safe enough,' observed the shocked Philip.

'You can bet any number of people are witnesses to financial transactions every day but nothing happens,' said Bill grimly. 'It must have been a set-up. Though you'd have thought this place would have been wise to that sort of thing.'

'I imagine the staff know the local rogues,' said Rebecca, 'you can't expect them to anticipate opportunist theft.'

'Besides,' said Ella, 'don't the police seem to think you were mugged by a tourist gang, not locals?'

'If that makes it any better,' said Oliver.

'Thanks to Oliver,' and Rebecca smiled at him warmly, 'I was rescued very quickly and it was such a help having him at the police station. The police were very kind but they're chauvinists, the lot of them.'

'Rebecca, you don't mean that,' expostulated Ella.

'Oh, yes I do. They'd only listen to Oliver. It was as though I wasn't there. And I was the victim,' she said indignantly.

'But you found them their man,' said Oliver, sitting beside her.

'So did you.'

'Rebecca recognized one of the men from a photograph.'

'And Oliver seems to have picked out our mystery third man.'

'I'd been talking to Jonah in the plaza. At the time I never gave it a thought, but there was this man who'd walked towards me very purposefully as I was making my way back. He'd not been running, or anything like that, but he was walking fast towards the town centre and stuffing something into the pocket of his jeans. He was having difficulty because they were so tight. I noticed that, so I suppose that's why I remembered him. Anyway, I recognized his photograph at the police station.'

'Interestin' that,' said Jonah. 'If you'd not stopped to be civil to me, you'd prob'ly bin in the hotel when she was mugged.'

There was a pause. Then Rebecca laughed. 'Good try, Jonah. OK, I'll buy it. I mean, obviously it was thanks to you Oliver was there to pick up the pieces, so I'll buy you dinner tonight.'

'Fanks, mate,' and he lifted his glass to her. 'You never know when you need a friend.'

# Chapter Fifteen

The previous day of rest notwithstanding, Ella decided she did not fancy walking through either the suburbs of León, or its rubbish dumps, scrap heaps and warehouses as described in their guide. Accordingly she arranged to meet them at the Sanctuary of the Virgen del Camino. Rebecca hesitated momentarily, then said she'd really prefer to walk and it was Jonah who went off with the older woman to find a taxi.

That night they discovered that the local refuge possessed a kitchen. They bought red wine which they drank while they chopped tomatoes, mushrooms, garlic and made a sauce and when it was ready they ate it under the stars with a vast pot of pasta.

They reached Astorga early the following afternoon, and there they stayed for an hour or two before going on to Murias de Rechivaldo, one of the old muleteer villages. Philip waxed lyrical over Astorga's neo-Gothic Bishop's Palace, but Ella said disparagingly she thought it was too much like something out of Disneyland for her taste, though she had liked the Camino room in the Museum of the Ways.

'Did anyone find the Celda de las Emparedadas?' Jonah asked. 'You must have looked for it, Bill.'

Bill shook his head. Ella regarded Jonah sternly. Questions asked in honeyed tones such as Jonah had used spelt trouble. 'If it had really been of interest, I am sure you would have mentioned it before,' she said repressively.

'So what was its importance, then?' asked Bill impatiently.

'It was where they locked up the local whores,' said Jonah.

'Traditionally pilgrims gave them part of their food as they passed by.'

'For a small consideration, I'll bet,' guffawed Philip. 'Sorry, Ella.'

'You can't mean they were running a municipal brothel?' said Rebecca. 'That's disgusting.'

'Oh, I don't know. . . .'

'I really wouldn't like to say,' said Jonah primly. 'I just thought Bill would—'

'You take far too much on yourself,' snapped Bill. 'Just mind your own damn business, will you?' There was a moment's shocked silence. They had heard Jonah goad Bill before, but never with this effect. Bill flushed. 'I'm sorry,' he mumbled.

'Silly young man,' said Ella to Jonah mildly. 'You simply must learn not to be offensive. Now I'm sure you have a more suitable story for us, if you think hard.'

Jonah shrugged. It was noticeable he did not apologize. 'I don't suppose anyone wants to walk another couple of kilometres tonight? No? I thought not,' to a chorus of groans. 'It's a pity in a way, because there's a village nearby where they make a meal that takes several days to prepare.'

'Why?' demanded Philip.

'How?' asked Rebecca.

He explained. 'It was during the time of the Peninsular Wars. Sir John Moore was fighting in the vicinity and he was expecting the French to attack at any time. He was in this inn and his dinner was ready and his officers said there was no sign of the French, but he ordered them to serve the best part of the meal first – that is, the meat – just in case they had to leave in a hurry. He ate the meat, but the French were nowhere in sight, so he demanded the vegetables. After that, when the French had still not arrived, he drank the soup that remained.'

'So you get a dinner in the reverse order?' observed Rebecca. 'Different.'

'It's more than that. They put everything into the stew, every kind of meat you can think of, which is why it takes so long to cook. The vegetable is mostly cabbage.'

'Some of the meat might end up a bit dry,' said Rebecca, 'but

I should imagine the soup is delicious.'

'But think of the walk back,' said Ella.

They had promised themselves a night in Rabanal del Camino for the Gaucelmo refuge had been rebuilt by the Confraternity of Saint James in England. It was simple, unadorned, almost unashamedly English with showers that actually threw hot water at you. It was also halfway up the mountain in front of them, Monte Irago.

Later that evening Oliver, sitting outside with a bottle of wine, got into conversation with one of the other pilgrims staying there, a well-spoken, middle-aged man, painfully thin with a pasty, puffy complexion and a way of looking at you as if he were short-sighted. He said his name was Peter and he'd been on the road for fourteen months.

'You must've had some fascinating experiences on the way,' said Oliver, not altogether sure he wanted to hear them but not churlish enough to get up and leave.

'Not really . . . well . . . I say, I've an empty glass here, and you seem to have an almost full bottle. How about the story of my life in exchange for a drop?'

'Why not,' agreed Oliver resignedly. 'Everyone else seems to have gone to bed.'

'If you're sitting comfortably, as they say,' said Peter with a companionable grin, a large swallow of the wine inside him, 'I'll begin. I started in Canterbury, fourteen months ago, and I've been walking more or less ever since.'

'That's quite a time,' interrupted Oliver. 'What's taken you. . . .' He stopped, suddenly aware that implying Peter walked extremely slowly would sound offensive. 'I mean, what made you do it? You must have a strong motivation, or something, to put up with this sort of life.' He, like the rest of the band, might not have started with the aspect of pilgrimage as his driving force, but it was impossible not to hear stories of pilgrim endurance, walk those relentless miles himself under that searing sky and not feel admiration for someone who was patently worse off than himself, older and assuredly less fit. 'Or shouldn't I ask?' he ended belatedly.

'That's fine by me,' replied Peter. 'I'm doing it for my congregation. A sort of collective pilgrimage, if you see what I mean.'

'Not entirely.'

'One Sunday we had a visit from a former pilgrim. What he told us really fired the imagination. Um. Well, actually, I was the vicar and I suddenly thought, this is what I've been waiting for all my life. A pilgrimage. One of the great pilgrimages.'

'How lucky you are,' exclaimed Oliver involuntarily, 'to have a vision to get you through all this.' He waved his hand towards the mass of the mountain before them, darker than the night sky.

'I don't see where luck comes into it.'

'I expect that's the wrong word. You see, for myself, I'm not really one of those on a pilgrimage as such.' Any more explanation seemed superfluous. 'Anyway, go on,' his interest in the man caught.

'I persuaded my bishop to give me leave of absence and he suggested I should look for a few companions. For company, support, that sort of thing. I gather there are several of you travelling together. That's where your luck comes in,' and he sounded wistful. 'Several of my parishioners thought they'd come with me – in fact they became very enthusiastic – but then, oh, you know, someone's wife got pregnant, someone else found he just couldn't get leave of absence from his job. It was too far, would take too long. . . .'

'All the usual excuses,' nodded Oliver.

'So in the end I said I'd do it for them, provided they sponsored me.'

'That was a novel suggestion. And obviously they were happy with it.'

'Oh, indeed they were,' said Peter a little bitterly. 'Unfortunately it's not worked out quite as it was intended. I mean,' he said, 'I shouldn't have taken quite so long to get this far.'

'Well . . . I expect most men of . . . I mean, I would probably have taken just as long.'

'You see, they promised to send me funds at regular intervals. This is the third time I've had to hang around waiting for the money to arrive.'

'You're joking.'

'I most certainly am not. Fortunately, the Confraternity knows what's happening and here they've been very good about it. Allowed me to stay while I'm waiting, on the understanding that my congregation eventually gives them a good donation.'

'Sounds reasonable enough. I daresay it could be awkward, though, if they weren't able to check on you. I suppose they might think you could be some sort of a conman.'

'You'd be amazed how many there are of those on the Camino,' said Peter darkly. 'Anyway, what I went through in France beggar's description. I was sleeping in church porches, ditches, you name it. I must have lost several stone because I couldn't afford to eat.'

'You do look a little thin,' said Oliver diplomatically.

Peter laughed as he stuck his hand in between the waistband of his torn and baggy shorts and his emaciated body. 'You can say that again. Though, to be fair, I was probably overweight before I started off. You know how it is.'

Excess weight had never been one of Oliver's problems. He merely smiled sympathetically. 'So what happens now?'

'I'm not sure. My churchwarden says they're having problems. He hopes something'll be forthcoming by the end of the week but he's not prepared to guarantee anything himself. You know, there are times when I've a good mind to pack it all in and go home.'

'You shouldn't do that,' exclaimed Oliver. There was a pause while he poured a little more wine for them both. That thought he'd had about what you did with a considerable amount of money earning interest while he was indulging himself. He would hate to offend, but. . . . 'Would a loan be of any help? I mean, don't take this the wrong way, but I'd like to help, if you would let me?'

'Help me with a loan?'

'I do realize you wouldn't want to take anything from another pilgrim that seemed like charity, but I could certainly manage – say fifty pounds?' He took his wallet out of his zipped back pocket. 'Actually, I could make it seventy-five. It's not that far to the next bank and I can manage perfectly well on what I have left,' he said, holding out a folded wad of notes. 'I really do want you to have this.'

With a fine show of reluctance, Peter took the money. 'Don't forget to give me your name and address,' he insisted. 'And if you write down your details, you know, the sort code of your bank and the account number, I'll get John – that's my church-warden – to make sure the money is repaid straight away. This is very kind of you,' he said. 'I know these things are often for the good of our soul, but you cannot imagine how frustrating it has been, watching everyone continue on the pilgrimage and being stuck here through no fault of my own. I'm sure God will bless you most warmly.'

Oliver tried not to wince. 'Thanks for the thought,' he said. He hesitated again. Wasn't there something about not advertising good deeds? 'Just one thing, Peter.'

'What is that?'

'I'd be grateful if you didn't mention any of this to the others. My friends, that is. It wouldn't really do.'

'My dear friend, I wouldn't dream of it. Well now, I am going to turn in and get a good night's sleep so that I can make an early start tomorrow, so I'll just say God bless, and I hope we meet again.'

'Peter.'

'Yes?'

'The rest of the wine. Would you. . . ?'

'Great. Thanks. It'll go down a treat tomorrow. Good night.'

Monte Irago was punishing. Rabanal del Camino to Ponferrada was also thirty-two kilometres away and after Monte Irago and with the prospect of more very hard walking ahead, everyone but Oliver declared that for one stage it was too long, so they decided to make for the basic mountain refuge at Manjarín – those who failed to find a bed for the night walking on to El Acebo.

'Are you sure you don't mind walking two easy days?' Rebecca asked Oliver, during the course of the morning. She had been sure he wanted to spend the day accepting the challenge, stretch his legs and storm ahead and something about his change of mind bothered her.

'Easy?'

She expelled a deep breath. 'You know what I mean.'

He chuckled. 'I had thought I might, but then I thought about the empty evening ahead and decided it wasn't worth it.'

'You'd have found someone to talk to. Bound to, especially being on your own. Like last night.'

'What about last night?' he asked sharply.

Rebecca raised her eyebrows, opened her mouth to say something, thought better of it. 'I saw you with one of the other pilgrims as I was going to bed.'

'He'd been on the road for some months,' Oliver answered cautiously. 'We swapped a few tales while we shared a bottle.'

'There you are, then,' she said smugly. 'If you are on your own, there is an incentive to make contact with other people. You try far harder than if you are with someone else.'

Oliver appeared to consider this. 'I'm not sure I tried all that hard last night,' he admitted, 'though in the end I found him interesting.'

'And there was the bottle to finish.'

'Exactly. Yet I don't always want to bother to find out who the interesting people are. Besides, one or other of us usually discovers them wherever we are staying.'

'Especially Ella.'

'She certainly has the knack. Remember the Australian journalist and her twin brother?' She was a photographer, and he wrote. They had both thrown up good jobs to travel the world, making their living by selling travel articles, and they planned to write a book together when they got home. 'Those travel writers were weird. They'd both left families behind, yet they seemed to hate each other.'

'Perhaps you do, after a while, if you're that close to start with, is that what you're saying?'

'I don't think I'm suggesting anything of the sort,' objected Oliver. 'And it's probably different for twins. But you do wonder why they should have embarked on such an experience unless they'd a good reason.'

'Mm. I think you've a very vivid imagination. So what are

you implying?' she persisted. 'That familiarity breeds contempt? That's an awful way of looking at life.' She paused. 'Though it happens to be true in my case.'

'You mean that's why your marriage failed? I'm sorry. I shouldn't be saying things like that to you of all people.' Inwardly he cursed himself for bringing up a subject she must be regretting she ever told him about, must want forgotten.

'I don't really know why it all happened as it did with my marriage,' Rebecca said honestly. 'And, before you ask, I don't mind discussing it. You see, at first Mike and I loved each other. We had a good life, especially when – when the children came. At least, that was what I believed. How wrong can you be?'

'It takes two—'

'Make or break a relationship. Well, of course I know that.'

'Rebecca, was there no suggestion that you should get back together?'

'When the children died? No. By then it was far too late. I think we both knew we had to stay apart for our own sanity. The memories were altogether too painful.'

'So you're footloose?'

'And fancy free,' she agreed. It was with considerable amazement that she realized all of a sudden that it wasn't altogether true. Somehow, at some time Oliver had crept a little too close to her. This unexpected revelation made her turn her ankle on the uneven surface of the track.

'Careful,' exclaimed Oliver, grabbing her arm. 'Watch where you're going. These stones are dire.'

'I was watching,' she answered crossly through confused feelings. 'Sorry. I was distracted thinking about something else.

The children. Of course she was, idiot that he was. 'Anyway, to get back to the subject of tonight,' he said hastily. 'I like travelling with a familiar group. I'm not particularly interested in seeking out the reasons why other people are doing what we are doing. So the Camino takes a little longer than I anticipated, so I'll go along with that and stick with the group. I'm no longer into doing things on my own.' It was an unlooked-for revelation. Moreover – my God, he thought in near panic – it was Rebecca he wanted to be with.

# Chapter Sixteen

At the same moment both Oliver and Rebecca stopped. It was then that they realized they had outstripped the others by a considerable distance. Talking about the others relieved the tension each was well aware had arisen between them – though each was vaguely aware that this tension had in it an altogether different element from anything they'd experienced before. They busied themselves finding a patch of grass growing under a boulder, conveniently situated in the shade by the side of the path and waited for them to catch up. Oliver swallowed several mouthfuls of water from the bottle on his waist and Rebecca rummaged in the small pocket of her backpack for a bag of mints. In a thoughtful silence they unwrapped the sweets and sucked on them, carefully folding the small squares of paper which they put back in the bag. Whatever, Oliver decided, nothing was going to happen between them so he might as well forget the whole thing – which was probably merely overwrought imagination anyway. He shifted his backpack more comfortably under his head, and closed his eyes. 'It's difficult to imagine another way of life now, isn't it? It seems as though we've never done anything else but walk. Do you think we'll ever adjust to normality again, or will we be nomads for the rest of our lives?'

Rebecca smiled. 'We've only been walking for a few weeks, but, yes, I do see what you're getting at. On the other hand. . . .' her voice trailed away. This relationship, such as it was, was going nowhere and she might as well get used to the idea, though how it even became an idea in her situation was a total puzzle.

'On the other hand, what?' he prompted her, opening his eyes and turning his head so that he might see her properly.

'Some of us have no choice but to get back to what we left behind as soon as possible after this has finished,' she pointed out.

Reconciling herself to the loss of her family, he thought uncomfortably. 'You shouldn't try to hurry things,' he said.

'Things?'

'The grieving process.'

'I know,' she replied quietly. 'But there is such as thing as a living to be made, whatever else has to be worked through.'

Knowing his own resources were likely to be considerably greater than hers or probably anyone else's on the pilgrimage, Oliver felt chastened. Then he said, 'So you do know what you are going to do, once we part in Santiago? Because I haven't a clue. I had this marvellous notion that there would be time on the walk for all sorts of deep, introspective thinking. You know, where I'm at, where I'm going, and so on.'

He paused and Rebecca said, 'I suppose you're right, in a way. I thought I'd be brooding a lot more than I am. I'm even sleeping better than I was at the beginning.'

'I know what you mean,' he said with deep feeling so that she looked at him a little puzzled. He meant, of course, the sleepless nights he'd gone through before the tumour was diagnosed. He continued, oblivious to her bewilderment, 'I've thought about the path, the scenery, what we ate the night before, where we're going to sleep, whether I should have fastened my damp socks to the outside of my pack to dry. That sort of thing. And by no means quite so succinctly.'

'Deep thoughts, though,' she smiled at him.

'I think I know where I'm at,' he said abruptly, 'but where I'm going . . . I have no more of a clue than when I started the Camino. Probably less, if you want the truth. So, what about you, Rebecca?' he said coaxingly. 'What will you do?'

Rebecca grimaced. 'Oh, I'll admit I thought I had it all planned, but somewhere along the line the plan seems to have suffered a jolt. Now I can't raise much enthusiasm for what I thought I wanted, even less for where I wanted to go.'

'And where was that?'

'Cornwall. It seemed such a good place to bring up children. Now I can hardly bear to think about it. I wanted a small restaurant of my own. That just seems too much of a hassle. Oliver, do you think the pilgrimage is a dreadful self-indulgence, that it has got such a hold on us we'll never, ever be the same again?' her voice broke a little.

Studiously he kept his eyes from her face. 'Of course we'll never be quite the same people again,' he answered after a moment. 'How could we be, unless we were dead from the neck up. And, whatever we are, I don't believe that of any of us. We've met people, done things we probably didn't think we were capable of, seen places we only imagined. Of course we've changed. So, logically our personal goal posts have shifted.'

'But where has all the energy gone, all the decisiveness some of you must have started with?'

'Gone into carrying heavy packs and putting one foot in front of the other, most like. Not that I had an abundance of energy to start with. After all, how many days' consecutive walking had you done before this?'

'Not a lot.'

'Quite. I expect we've all got calluses on our shoulders where we never thought to find them,' he grinned and rubbed his right shoulder reflectively. 'You know,' he continued, 'when Bill – I suppose it was Bill – said we ought to have regular days to rest, I thought he was being super-cautious. I went along with it because I wanted to stay with the group, but I had such plans to do side trips on my own – or with anyone who wanted to come with me. And have I?' he shrugged. 'One or two in the beginning, but now, now I do some washing and that's about all.'

'Conserving your energy.'

'That's it.'

'Which I suppose is all we can do. But it doesn't help, when it comes to knowing what to do next. So what are you going to do, Oliver?'

'I told you. I haven't the least idea. Only what I don't want to do.'

'Which is? That is, if you don't mind talking about it,' she said diffidently. How much more of a complex man he was than she had given him credit for, she was thinking. What was there in his past that had made him what he was?

He stood up. 'No sign of the others yet. Actually, putting things into words might even help the thought processes.' He hesitated. Rebecca had taken him very much on trust by telling him about her children. She deserved better than a contrived concealment from him. 'You see,' he said eventually as she sat very still, as if she were willing him to confide in her, 'for a time I was ill.'

'I knew it,' she said involuntarily.

'How did you know?' he frowned.

'You looked very pale, at that first meeting in the pub. Not pale, somehow drained. What happened, Oliver?' Whatever it was she thought, the truth – and he told her everything – surprised her. 'But that's marvellous, to be cured.'

'It could just be a remission.'

'And that's defeatist talk.'

'I know. Most of the time I try to be positive. Thinking what to do with my life now, though, is one of the hardest things to do.'

'I can imagine that.'

'For instance, I don't want to go back into money-making,' he said, stretching, then flexing his legs.

'Lucky for some that's no problem,' she said drily.

He grinned. 'I meant that I won't return to the financial world. That's where I've been since I left university one way or another.'

'Which way, exactly?' she probed daringly.

'Too long a story,' he replied briefly.

'Sorry.'

'Don't be. Some day I'll tell you all about it.'

She absorbed that. So many revelations at one session implied their relationship would – might improve to an incalculable degree. 'So you don't exactly have to earn too much to live on?' she said cautiously.

'More or less. I can't say I'm very keen on commerce in any form nowadays, if it comes to a way of life.'

'The professions? Medicine, the law, teaching?'

Oliver groaned. 'Couldn't take coping with people's everyday ills. Couldn't possibly do the studying required for law. Wouldn't have the patience to deal with disaffected youth. See what a hopeless case I am?'

'Perhaps you should grow things?'

'Somehow I don't see myself as a farmer, either.'

'Well, perhaps that does mean an awful lot of early mornings and hard, manual work,' she agreed light-heartedly.

'Now you're taking the mickey.' He came and sat down beside her again.

'Only a little. Perhaps you should decide where you want to live and then work out how to achieve it.'

Oliver forbore to say all he had to do was sign a cheque. He knew it wasn't what she meant at all. He'd not seen her so animated for some time. Not since before the incident in the lift. He had grown to like the new, quieter, softer Rebecca but in a strange way he missed the spiky, acerbic woman and the almost predictable way they had struck sparks off each other. And there was a serious edge to this conversation, forcing him to think about things he had let drift to the back of his consciousness. 'Not London, or the Home Counties,' he declared.

'No. Don't tell me where you don't want to live, Oliver. Be more positive.'

He shrugged. 'One of the Scottish islands, perhaps. The Outer Hebrides. It's a beautiful part of the world.'

'That'd be all right if you were a crofter.'

'I could take up weaving. Or knitting.'

'Be serious.'

'I am being serious. Mid-Wales, then. What could I do in Mid-Wales?'

'Sheep?'

'As in keep sheep? I don't know the first thing about them.'

'Chickens, then.'

'The clucking would drive me mad.'

'Pigs, bees, tourists. . . .'

'Do you know, I've always had a hankering to do that, one day.'

'Tourists?'

'No, keep bees.'

'Grow honey?'

'Something tells me you've not spent much time in the country,' he said. 'Grow honey,' he scoffed.

'Well, you know what I mean. But have you? Spent much time in the country? What do you know about keeping bees?'

'I've a farming background, but I don't know a great deal about bees,' he admitted. 'Though I had a godmother who kept half-a-dozen hives. It always fascinated me. I remember saying that one day, when I was as old as she was – or maybe seemed then – I'd have a hive or two at the bottom of my garden.'

'There you are,' Rebecca declared triumphantly. 'Buy a house with a large garden and keep bees, but maybe somewhere reasonably clement in the winter.'

'And what do I do with all my honey?'

'Sell it to tourists.'

'The same tourists you want to cook for? That could be interesting.'

Rebecca made a face. 'The trouble is, I don't think I've the energy to cook for tourists any more.'

Philip rounded a bend in the path. 'Hello, you two. You look very comfortable there.'

Oliver stretched. 'We were. I highly recommend it for ten minutes or so, but I think my muscles are about to seize up so I'm going to leave you to it and carry on. Coming, Rebecca?'

'I need a bush first. I'll catch you up.'

The basic mountain refuge was no more than it claimed to be. But having passed through two deserted villages, the band had also failed to buy provisions for an evening meal. Pooling their combined resources did not yield more than a third of a bar of chocolate each, a quarter of an apple and half a stale roll.

'Oh, well,' said Philip philosophically, 'I guess we're better off than some.'

'Count yer blessings an' all that?' said Jonah.

'We are all in good health and we're far from starving,' said Bill sharply.

Ella said soberly, 'I think it must be extremely difficult to walk the Camino alone. We are very fortunate.'

'Oliver was saying something like that this morning.'

'So what's brought on this bout of soul searching?' asked Jonah.

Avoiding Oliver's eyes Rebecca said, 'The man running the refuge last night was telling me about a sad case he'd come across. Not just sad, I suppose. One of those conmen working the Camino. I imagine you could succumb to all sorts of temptations on a very long journey like this. Especially if you are on your own with only your own resources behind you.'

'You mean the druggie?' asked Jonah. They all exclaimed in varying degrees of surprise. 'I don't think you need to waste your sympathies too much on him,' Jonah continued. 'He picks his victim carefully, brings out the sob stuff about having no money, you know, changes the story to suit his victim. Set upon by local yobs, money hasn't been sent by wicked wife, spent it all on medical treatment because he's not entitled to the P111 form. Occasionally he even pretends to be an ordained priest whose congregation has failed to come across.'

'You make it sound as though it's lucrative,' said Philip. 'People fall for this?'

'Regularly,' said Jonah. 'You see, he looks the part. Thin, ill. Of course the reason for that is the drugs. That's what he spends the money on.'

'And he gets away with it?' said Ella. 'Truly amazing.'

'Though I guess most of his victims aren't aware they've been conned,' said Philip charitably.

'And when they do learn about it they are probably too embarrassed to confess they've been had so the authorities don't stand a chance of catching the man,' commented Rebecca shrewdly.

'So what's wrong with that?' demanded Oliver. 'There's a lot worse in this world than being had by a con man.'

'That's what I meant about temptation,' said Rebecca. 'Charitably disposed pilgrims falling for a tall story. Conman getting away with it because when his victim does realize what has happened it's all too much to find someone to deal with it.'

'Sittin' ducks,' said Jonah. 'Suppose no one's got any wine?

Thought not. Oh, well, I guess it'll just have to be water.'

In Ponferrada, so called from the eleventh-century iron bridge built over the River Sil for the use of pilgrims on the orders of the Bishop of Astorga, the band settled for modest, two-star accommodation. There was no refuge, but their guide book promised that pilgrims would be looked after by locals in '*a brotherly manner*.' Jonah went off to find it.

It was the next day that he fell in step with Oliver.

'How much the druggie sting you for, then?' he asked casually, after they'd walked in silence for a while.

'What the. . . . How. . . ?'

'Did I know?' Jonah shrugged. 'S'easy, really. You looked more shifty'n usual when you was talkin' 'bout conmen.'

'Rude bugger.'

'Me or him? You don't have to answer that. So what story did he pull on you?'

Oliver sighed. 'Parish priest persuaded to take sabbatical and go on pilgrimage for sake of congregation. Unfeeling parishioners renege on agreement to subsidize priest. Poor pilgrim half-starves. Come to think of it I'm surprised it wasn't the set-upon-by-local-yobs story he used for me, though I suppose he realized I didn't know much about the workings of your average parish. I offered seventy-five.'

'Blimey, mate. Why you do that?'

'I don't know. Well, yes I do. It seemed a good idea, at the time. It was only a loan,' he added defensively. Then Oliver swore again. 'I also gave him the number of my bank account. You don't suppose he. . . . No. I think the bank'd have more sense than to pay out on my account.'

'But you're thinking you'd better contact them, all the same?'

'I presume having nasty suspicious thoughts about the man cancels out the brownie points I gained for being charitable,' Oliver said wryly.

'I guess not. You don't seem too outraged. I thought you would have been.'

'Oh, I enjoyed the warm glow. You know. By the way, how did you get on, last night?'

'Thanks for asking. I was given a pongy mattress on the floor of a derelict summer house.'

'Is that all?'

'There were rats.'

'Give you anything to eat, did they?'

'That's what the rats were after. They were welcome to it. It certainly wasn't fit to save for lunch today.'

'Oh, well, win some, lose some. At least you'd had a decent dinner. Jonah?'

'What?'

'You won't mention anything of what happened to me to anyone, will you?'

'Anyone as in Rebecca? I wouldn't be surprised if she hasn't already guessed.'

'I wouldn't want her to take me for a complete fool.'

'I doubt if she'd do that. Fancy her, don't you?'

'What do you mean?'

'Come on. S'a bit obvious, you know.'

'I don't think you know anything of the sort,' said Oliver stiffly.

'Well, I don't intend to offend,' said Jonah.

'In case I opt out of the my-turn-to-pay rota? Sorry. That was offensive.'

'Yeah. Well, I probably deserve it. Anyway, about Rebecca.' Oliver stiffened. 'I was just going to say that if she has guessed about you and the druggie I don't think she'll ever mention it, do you?'

# Chapter Seventeen

They were on their way to Villafranca del Bierzo. The day was oppressively hot but thunder clouds that gathered in the late morning in the west disappeared to leave a fine afternoon as they emerged from dense vegetation on to a wider track called the Camino de la Virgen.

'There's another Puerta del Perdón along here,' Jonah told them all as they regrouped. 'It's at the Romanesque Church of Santiago.'

'What's a whatever-it-is?' asked Philip.

'A door of pardon,' Ella answered promptly. 'Jonah told me about the door in León. I made sure I touched that one.'

'Superstitious nonsense,' grunted Bill.

'But what is it for?' asked Oliver. 'I don't remember anything about it.'

'In the fifteenth century, Pope Calixto III, who was Spanish, granted absolution and plenary indulgence to pilgrims who reached Villafranca on their way to Compostela but were unable to go any further.'

'Obviously the longer they'd been walking, the more injuries the pilgrims would have suffered,' said Ella. 'The old, the very young and the frail often died on the road. The nearer we get to Santiago the more roadside graves we shall see. Lead me to the door, I'm not wasting any opportunity.'

Rebecca grimaced. 'I hadn't thought about what it must have felt like to be one of the early, believing pilgrims who was forced to abandon the journey. I should be upset myself if I had to give up now. Can you imagine the crushing disappointment a real pilgrim would feel if he, or she, failed close to Compostela?'

'Graves,' said Philip. 'I'd not thought of those.'

'Where else would you find them,' commented Ella, 'except by the roadside.'

'Grue-some,' mocked Jonah.

'It is nonsense, though,' said Bill, 'especially the belief in indulgences.'

'Is it?' replied Jonah. 'I'd have called it charity, meself.'

Villafranca was beautifully set in a valley between four high mountains and at the confluence of two rivers, and there they booked into the parador for two nights. 'They say the refuge is one of the most friendly along the Camino,' Ella, who had heard about the rats, said to Jonah. 'So you should be all right tonight. But come and have dinner with us as usual.'

The next day those who needed to rest sat around and did very little. Others washed and shopped and Jonah and Oliver did the historical sites of the town, which, with its valley situation was hot and stifling. In mid-afternoon there were even a few rumbles of thunder.

'It would be a relief if we had a storm tonight,' said Oliver, running a finger round the inside of the collar of his shirt.

'But I don't think we're going to,' said Jonah. He hoped not. The refuge was certainly friendly – there had been an impromptu party into the small hours. It had also been famously described by Nicholas Luard as '*smelling of cat's pee and otter droppings*', and once the party was over Jonah had dragged his sleeping bag outside under a tree. If it rained tonight he'd have to make other arrangements.

They had decided that they would try to do the following stage, Villafranca to O Cebreiro, 27.8 kilometres and high in the mountains, in one day. The map showed that from Villafranca the route diverged, the original path following the N V1 along the valley bottom, a busy road full of heavy lorries and unsafe for pilgrims who had to walk right by the traffic. The preferred route now climbed the Cerro del Real into unspoilt countryside, a much tougher walk but with splendid views over the valley below. Both paths met at the village of

Trabadelo. Ella said she'd take a local taxi and meet up with them in the village. The others trudged up the hill towards the Barrio de Tejedores to discover a telling Camino image on a wall in front of a church, a mural of pilgrims in traditional garb pointing the way onward with their pilgrim staves, strikingly bold blue-black figures on a beige-washed background, which Philip very much admired.

The lane they were in was quiet and Oliver and Rebecca were walking abreast. Bill was way ahead and Philip had dropped back for a call of nature. Behind and talking animatedly were Ella and Jonah. 'Strange young man, that,' commented Oliver. 'You'd think he'd prefer the company of people his own age, yet he stays with us. And I don't think it's just because of the free dinners.'

'Sometimes I wonder just how old he is,' said Rebecca.

'And that is an odd remark.'

'He seems to have an old soul.'

'Ah,' said Oliver. 'Are we going to talk about the state of our souls, then?'

'Not likely. I'm not sure I'm into that sort of thing.'

'You mean you don't believe in souls, or life after death and all that?'

'I think I must do,' said Rebecca defensively, 'or I wouldn't be on this walk. I would like nothing better than to believe implicitly that some day I'll see Charley and Toby again. But will I? I don't know, I just haven't decided one way or the other.' The conversation was threatening to become heavy. She said determinedly, 'I think it's a bit like your bees, leaving it until I'm older. What about you?'

'Mm,' said Oliver. 'I think we might be on dangerous ground there. Like you, I'm an undecided, I think.' She smiled. 'OK. Let's change the subject. You sorted me out the other day, about the bees.'

'You mean that's what you're going to do?'

'Don't sound so surprised. Actually I haven't quite decided, but it's not a bad idea. So, when we were interrupted, I was about to pin you down.'

'Not literally, I hope,' she muttered primly.

He shot her an odd look. 'Too public,' he said briefly. 'I really meant that I was about to go back to what you'd said about no longer wanting to cook for tourists.'

'Oh, I guess I probably will, eventually. If only because I need to earn my living and that's the way I do it best. It's just that I look at Jonah – all the young people, I suppose – who have time to take out before buckling down to the serious part of life. I never did that. Did you, Oliver?'

'No. I went straight into making money. That gave me all the buzz I needed at the time. Now, well, I no longer need either to make money or to seek a buzz. Been there, done that, I guess.'

'Old before your time.'

'More like burnt out,' he said soberly.

'I know I have to move on, even though I've resisted accepting that I must. But instead of buying my own business immediately, I thought I might travel a bit.'

Oliver groaned theatrically. 'Don't tell me, do your thing in India. Go vegetarian and fall at the feet of a guru. And get some parasitical disease that'll make you sallow-skinned and as thin as a rake. And all your hair will drop out. Oh dear.'

'Not at all, and anyway I really don't think that's my thing. Besides, I can't afford more than an indirect route to New Zealand. When I get there I'll work for someone else until I've made up the shortfall, then decide where to buy a business.'

'In New Zealand?'

'That's what I thought.'

'It's a good place. A long way from home, though.'

'That's the trouble. It is far. I do realize I won't see Charley and Toby grow up but I don't know if I can bear to live so far away from. . . .' She gulped, reached for a handkerchief and blew her nose.

Oliver, thwarted by the backpack from putting an arm round her shoulder – which he wanted to do quite desperately – placed his hand gently on the nape of Rebecca's neck. 'Do you know, you are about the only woman I know who always has a hankie?'

She gave a spontaneous giggle, but she did not move away, he noticed.

'And you could always cut your losses and come home, if you didn't like it, after all,' he added.

'I'm not too proud to admit defeat, no. As for coming home. . . .' Her voice trailed. His hand was comforting and she was unaccountably dismayed when he took it away. She turned to look at him and he saw that her eyes were wet.

After a moment he said, 'What do you see, when you settle down.'

'I don't understand.'

'You've talked about the job, where it might be. Do you see yourself always alone?'

'You mean, will I ever have another serious relationship again? Who knows?' She shrugged. 'If it happens maybe I shall count myself lucky. I'm not so sure I'm not too much like bad luck for someone else to take on. Far too much emotional baggage for it to be fair for any man to take me on.'

'How ridiculous,' and he sounded as though he meant it.

'Well,' said Rebecca. There was a pause. 'What about you, Oliver?'

'At a bit of a loose end, I suppose. Not into relationships.' There was another pause. 'Not sure I'm all that lucky to be with. Defensive with it but just healthy enough to contemplate the Camino.'

'You're doing it as a thank you for still being here?'

'Not really. I don't know that I had a motive other than it was a challenge I believed I could overcome.'

'I wonder how many of us have deeply disguised reasons for coming on the Camino. Or if we shall ever know?'

They were becoming too introspective. Oliver did not want to make her sad again. He changed the subject abruptly. 'When you get to New Zealand, you don't have to buy a business, like a restaurant. You should first think about making a home, and then use your talents to take money from tourists.'

'Tourists again. How do I do that?' She let the bit about a home pass.

'Take people like us. Anywhere in the world where people are on the move. What do they, *we* need?'

'A bed, a meal. Tell me.'

'Bed and breakfast,' he answered triumphantly, as if no one else had ever thought of it before. 'Somewhere to hang wet clothes, or wash sweaty ones. An evening meal.'

'Sounds a bit of a hassle. But go on.'

'Find a tourist area you like. Buy a nice house, with enough room for paying guests, a decent dining-room. I think you'd find it wouldn't be long before you were sharing it with someone else, even if only a friend. You'd not be alone for long, you're not the type.'

'What type am I?' she asked cautiously.

'Caring, approachable, friendly.'

'Come on, Oliver, we're talking about me, remember. Rebecca. There was a time when you'd never have said that.'

'More fool me. I saw through the veneer, didn't I, in the end.'

Rebecca sighed. 'You could say you caught me at a vulnerable moment, I suppose.'

Dangerous ground, again, Oliver thought. 'I see you doing country house catering,' he backtracked. 'B and B. You could feed the locals at the weekend.'

'Thanks. I'll bear it in mind.'

'You know,' he said daringly, 'when you set your mind to it, I believe he wouldn't be too far away, someone you'd care for enough to have another relationship with.'

'No?'

They had come to a sudden halt, were standing gazing deep into each other's eyes, a look of perplexity on Rebecca's face, something akin to surprise on Oliver's.

What an extraordinarily intimate conversation, Rebecca was thinking. How could she have let this man come so close? Closer than she'd ever allowed Mike, even in those far-off early days of heady lust when they could not have enough of each other which she'd assumed signified undying love. She saw now that with Mike there had always existed an indefinable barrier between them. There was something about Oliver that was disarmingly compelling. If she let herself, there could come a time when. . . . Deliberately Rebecca blanked that thought out.

What an extraordinary woman Rebecca was, Oliver was thinking. There was something about her that he'd not encountered in any woman before, a warmth, a sympathy that was very endearing. It was not at all what he had expected from her.

'There's the way mark,' and Philip tapped Oliver on the shoulder. 'Couldn't you see it? It's right in front of your nose.'

'Way mark?' said Oliver distantly. 'Oh, yes. I hadn't noticed.'

'We were discussing the tourist trade,' said Rebecca vaguely.

'Tourist trade?' said Philip in the tone of voice that suggested he didn't believe a word of it. 'Must have been an absorbing conversation. I thought you were lost, not just lost to the world.'

'Well, you know,' said Rebecca brightly, 'we were comparing ourselves with your average tourist.'

'You couldn't possibly,' said Philip. 'There's just no comparison.'

'That's what we decided,' agreed Rebecca.'

'Oh, I see,' said Philip, mystified.

'Which was when you tapped me on the shoulder. Onward, then. Onward.' And Oliver turned on his heel and strode ahead.

# Chapter Eighteen

There were several punishing climbs that day, made more strenuous by a path paved with enormous flagstones and separated by deep declavities, and by the hot, airless day. And when they were high, there were the mountains, etched against grey-black clouds that menaced all morning but which continued to hover where they had been for three days.

But then the wind changed.

It began with a few spots of warm rain and for a while they thought the worst of the weather was going to pass them by. They were wrong. They regrouped while they were scrambling into wet-weather gear, state of the art stuff, with the exception of Jonah who produced a cape and a wide brimmed waterproof hat.

'What on earth is that?' expostulated Bill.

'The hat? An akubra. It's what the Aussie stockmen wear.'

'Fat lot of good it'll do you up here.'

'I don't know,' said Philip, chuckling. 'At least he won't be sweating under layers of fabric. So long as the wind doesn't get up even the hat'll probably stay on.'

'If it does we shouldn't complain,' said Ella. 'All these weeks we've had of unbridled sunshine, a bit of wind and rain won't kill us.'

'Are you going to be all right, Ella?' asked Oliver anxiously. 'I don't think we're going to have just rain. I think we're in for that storm that passed us by yesterday.'

Rebecca shivered. 'Rain doesn't bother me,' she said, 'thunder does.'

'Then you'd better stay close to her, Oliver,' said Ella. 'Things are never quite so bad when you have company.'

Bill had been consulting the guide book. 'We passed a municipal refuge at Vega de Valcarce,' he said. 'I reckon we're about halfway between that and O Cebreiro, if anyone's interested in going back down. I should imagine you'd get to shelter rather quicker than we will by going on.'

'And have to do all that climbing again tomorrow? Not me,' said Philip.

'I'd rather go on,' agreed Ella.

'Right,' said Bill. 'I'd prefer that we stayed together, too. Now, we've got another couple of kilometres to Laguna de Castilla, the last village in the province of León, and another kilometre beyond that there's the boundary marker between Castile and Galicia. On it is the distance to Santiago de Compostela, which, for your information, is 152 kilometres. From then on, there are stones every five hundred metres.'

'A countdown?' exclaimed Rebecca. 'How comforting.'

'We certainly shouldn't get lost, even in a storm,' agreed Bill, and as if on cue, a jagged flash of lightning flashed across the mountain tops.

'. . . seventeen, eighteen, nineteen, twenty,' chanted Ella. 'It's someway off yet.'

Philip shook his head indulgently. 'Come on, Ella. Let's get going. Just fix your mind on something hot and warming. . . .'

'Like a brandy,' said Rebecca, her teeth beginning to chatter.

Oliver took her hand. 'Philip's right. Let's get moving.'

The rain fell relentlessly, driving rain that chilled faces and hands, from massing clouds that began to blot out the mountains and the surrounding scenery until all that was visible between the vivid lightning flashes was the winding path ahead.

Counting seconds between flashes had been a childhood habit of Ella's. To encourage herself – because it was the lightning she most feared – Ella began counting with each flash. Five miles did not seem too bad, but two was too close for comfort. Getting nearer. A mental picture of the foil blanket she carried in her backpack – which itself had a metal frame – and both of which were likely to attract these forces of nature came into her mind. She saw herself transfixed by a bolt of lightning, lying dead on the path – at the very least badly wounded – and she moaned, though in those conditions no one heard her. No one would have heard her – for Ella was now walking some way behind everyone else. Ten paces off she saw two large boulders with just enough space between them for a person to shelter. Hurriedly, and with hands that shook, Ella took off her backpack – blessed relief – left it by the side of the path and squeezed between the boulders. As she did so the most brilliant flash of lightning yet illuminated the path and almost simultaneously thunder crashed overhead. Ella moaned again and crouched lower, praying for the earth to swallow her up.

'What a storm,' exulted Oliver who, true to say, had almost enjoyed the battle with the elements. 'For a while back there I almost thought we weren't going to make it. Here, let me take your anorak and hang it up.'

'You thought we weren't going to make it? I was petrified.'

'I suspected you were. You were shaking like a leaf at one time.'

'When the storm was right overhead.'

'All the same, it is the lightning that is the most dangerous.'

'I know. I just don't like the noise. Oliver, was that why you made me take off my backpack?' He nodded. 'Thanks, anyway.'

'My pleasure' As indeed he found that it was. Once again Rebecca had demanded, and secured, his protection. He'd certainly not minded. In fact, he'd actually enjoyed knowing that she felt safer with his arm round her (though what protection his arm would have done had lightning actually struck, he did not know).

One by one the others entered the refuge, exclaiming about what they saw as an adventure – now that it was over – shaking the wetness off their anoraks.

'But where is Ella?'

It did not take long to check she was not in the building, nor had she slipped into the old Church of Santa María la Real to light one of its scores of candles in their red holders. Oliver reached for his anorak and Rebecca, scared for him, and on her own account if they had to go back out once more into the storm that had by no means abated, struggled into hers.

'I'll go,' said Jonah. 'Ella can't have strayed off the path. I guess she's sheltering.'

'But. . . ?'

'You stay with Rebecca. Besides, it'll be less embarrassing for her if only one of us goes looking for Ella.' It was with no little surprise that they saw the door of the refuge close behind him. And no one followed.

'Santiago to the rescue,' muttered Bill ironically.

No one denied it. They were all thinking how very persuasive Jonah could be. At times, almost adamant.

'Ella'll be all right,' said Rebecca fearfully. 'Won't she?'

'. . . three, four, five . . . that's better,' Ella muttered to herself, and heaved a sigh of relief. There had only been two instantaneous flashes of lightning and claps of thunder since she had taken shelter behind the boulders, lightning which had still imprinted an angry rainbow of colour behind her tightly closed eyes and noise that left her ears ringing. Then for seconds there was only the sound of the rain. The next clap of thunder sounded almost benign as it rumbled several miles away and Ella's breathing slowly returned to normal.

The rain was not going to go away quite so quickly as the storm. She'd better get moving, she thought. No doubt the others had managed to find some shelter while the storm raged overhead – at least she fervently hoped so for their sakes, even if it was only a ditch. Being caught in the open would not have been nice. Then she wondered if anyone had been foolish enough to shelter under a tree – but there were not too many of those at this height, so probably her fears were groundless.

Concentrate, said Ella to herself, and grunted audibly as she found herself lodged between the boulders. With difficulty she eased herself back into the space she had occupied during the storm, turned, and attempted to sidle her way back to the path. Without success. 'This is ridiculous,' Ella said loudly, and tried again. Why it was so, she could not say, nor how she had managed to squeeze between the boulders in the first place, but now she was there she seemed to be imprisoned. She crouched: her shoulders were too wide even for the slightly larger gap at ground level. She wondered if she might climb out: the boulders were concave and she was no rock climber. 'Oh, sugar,' she said crossly, 'now what do I do?'

Afterwards, Ella maintained that she was never in any fear of being abandoned to a cold, wet fate. She knew someone would come. Inadvertently she had also done the correct thing and left her backpack by the side of the path. Too often people left the path for something simple, like a pee, and fell into a hole or did something equally stupid, and no one knew where they were until it was too late, but her backpack was where she had left it because of the lightning. Unfortunately so was her foil blanket and her whistle. 'Oh, well,' said Ella philosophically, 'someone is bound to come, soon.'

It was a long hour. She nibbled a square of chocolate that she discovered in one of her pockets, felt a bit sleepy after that and thought about curling up for a nap. Just as she was beginning to drift off she began to wonder how many others had taken shelter behind these boulders, wild animals, well, small wild animals, reptilian creatures, like snakes. She sat bolt upright. Snakes were wary creatures, she'd always believed. They wouldn't bother you if you didn't bother them, if they knew you were there. Noise. She'd sing. '*Save us, heavenly Father, save us . . .*' came first. Then it was, '*Onward, Christian soldiers, onward as to war. . . .*' Much more appropriate. She sang that twice, all the way through. '*Nobody knows de trouble I'm in, nobody knows but Jesus . . .*' or was it, '*trouble I've seen. . .* ?' She sang it both ways. '*Go down Moses, way down in Egypt land . . .*' was a good one for keeping up the spirits. She'd a larger repertoire than she realized. '*He who would valiant be. . . .* They ought to sing that at journey's end. If they reached Compostela. She fell silent.

They had spent time looking for her at the hostel and in the church before realizing Ella was truly missing. Then Jonah had gone back along the path slowly, anxious lest he miss her by hurrying past. Finding her backpack was an enormous relief. He thought he'd heard singing just before he found the backpack but when he stopped to listen it was quiet except for the sound of the rain dropping on the path and the wind ruffling the leaves on the hedge beside it. 'Ella. Ella!' There was no reply. Jonah frowned. There were two boulders by the path. One was an easy climb. He thought that from the top of it he might have some idea where she had gone. 'Dammit, she can't have gone far,' he muttered as he scrambled to his feet on top of it. 'Ella!'

The figure that loomed over her, darkening the small strip of sky above her head had something of the surreal about it, a pilgrim from medieval times, heavily cloaked with a wide-brimmed hat. 'Santiago,' Ella gasped. All he lacked was his staff. But he wouldn't want his staff on top of the boulder. She'd always known someone would come. She'd not expected this. 'Santiago,' she whispered, her hands clasped as if in prayer. And in the same breath he repeated, 'Ella.' His voice was soft, gentle reassuring as it penetrated the gloom of her prison.

He moved and a spattering of water drops fell on to her upturned face. 'Jonah,' Ella said. 'Good lord. For a moment I thought. . . . I seem to be stuck.'

'Silly woman. You've given us such a fright.'

'Then help me out of here, stupid boy, before I catch my death of cold.'

'That's it. That's gratitude for you. . . .'

Not for the first time Ella was struck by the two personas of Jonah, the callow youth, the almost-mystic.

It was not going to be easy. Jonah thought one of the boulders must have shifted, settled, somehow. In the end he decided she would have to be hauled out of the space. 'Only I'm not going to be able to do it on my own.'

'Too heavy for you, am I?'

'Not strong enough,' he admitted. 'Look, Ella, I've got to go back and get help. Anything in that pack of yours to keep you warm?'

'My foil blanket.'

He passed it through the gap to her along with a thin sweater and a scarf she had forgotten she was carrying. 'We'd better leave the backpack on the path to make sure we find you. This time I'll run. Be as quick as I can. . . .'

'My whistle. . . .' But he had gone. 'Oh well,' said Ella. '*He who would valiant be*,' she sang, ' '*gainst all disaster*. . . .' But this time the key was definitely major.

The others had waited for half an hour before deciding to set off after Jonah. 'No point in sitting here for Jonah to show up. For all we know, the same thing has happened to him as happened to Ella. We should never have let him go out on his own in this.'

They explained to the proprietor what had occurred and within minutes two more men from the hostel had joined their group to form a search party, well equipped with ropes, torches and something that looked suspiciously like a rolled-up stretcher. It was then that they began to feel really anxious. 'Accidents happen all too frequently in the mountains. Not just among the pilgrims who are walking through. It pays to be ready,' said the proprietress. 'But your friend will be cold. She must go straight to bed. I shall have bottles put there for her and hot soup waiting.'

A rope was needed. Ella was unable to climb out unaided, even with it, so Jonah, as the lightest, jumped into the space to help her. But she declined the stretcher. A brisk walk back would get her circulation going, she insisted. Brisk was perhaps not quite the word to use under the circumstances, but the Ella who entered the hostel was in a lot better shape than they had expected. She thanked the local men, insisted they had a drink at the bar and seemed all set to join them before Oliver laid down the law and led her upstairs.

'I know. I'm a silly old woman who's nothing but a nuisance.'

'Nonsense. It could have happened to any one of us. Something nastier still could. Anyway, you've no bones broken and if you get to bed now you probably won't even catch a cold.'

'You're quite right. A hot water bottle. Such luxury. Thank you, Oliver.'

'I'll fetch your supper.'

They had always intended staying in Cebreiro for two nights and in truth everyone, except Jonah, was relieved, because the weather had closed in on them, the rain continuing unabated. It was cold and visibility was limited. It also meant that unfortunately the hostel was going to be full. But hearing that it was Jonah who had been instrumental in rescuing Ella the previous evening, it was decided that since there were beds available, he might stay in the refuge for a second night. 'Tell you what, folks,' he confided to them at breakfast, 'this refuge has washing machines as well as hot showers.'

Since earliest times, the pilgrims' hospital at Cebreiro had been one of the most important along the Camino. A miracle had occurred at Cebreiro – which Bill, unexpectedly, had told them about while the group was waiting for Jonah to find Ella the previous evening.

'It happened in the early fourteenth century,' Bill related, 'during a snowstorm. A peasant from a nearby village battled through the dreadful conditions just so he might receive communion. The priest felt nothing but contempt for this simple soul who could easily have stayed at home, but while he was administering the sacrament the bread and wine turned into the actual flesh and blood of Christ.'

'You doin' a Jonah on us?'

'I don't know what you mean, Philip.'

'You sounded just like the boy.'

'Or maybe he read the same guidebook.'

'Maybe I did.' For a moment Bill had looked angry, then he managed a wintry smile. 'Anyway, if anyone is interested, the paten and chalice used at the time are kept in the church next door.'

Cebreiro was also noted for its pallozas, straw-roofed single-storey houses, unchanged since prehistoric times. One was being converted near the refuge and two more were the village's museum.

By the following morning the storm was nothing but a memory, with the sky washed clean, the air fresh and heady, so that you could see for miles. They set off once more refreshed and eager. Yet there was one sour note. Rebecca and Ella were the first ready and they waited together on the cobbles outside the hostel.

Rebecca said, 'You seem sprightly enough this morning after

your adventure, but are you sure you're doing the right thing?'

'You mean, am I sure I'm not going to crack up on you some time today?'

'Well, something of the sort. I wouldn't have put it quite like that.' Nor should she, Rebecca thought, too late and totally dismayed by the look of downright anger on Ella's face. 'I mean,' she went on, compounding the felony, 'you gave us all such a scare, getting lost like that. And you must have been very frightened. It's a miracle you didn't catch pneumonia.'

'Have you quite finished?' Rebecca was silenced. 'Firstly, I didn't get lost, as you describe it. I knew exactly where I was. Secondly, I wasn't in the least frightened. Not once the storm passed and probably no more than you were during it. Thirdly, there was no chance of contracting pneumonia. I was sensibly clad in waterproofs. I had a foil blanket to save me from hypothermia. I arrived at the hostel chilled but bone dry and I took care of the chill by going to bed with hot soup and a glass of red wine. The fact that I became stuck behind two boulders and had to be rescued was unfortunate, I admit, but it could have happened to anyone.'

'I didn't mean—'

'Oh, yes, I rather think you did, young woman. However, there haven't been many occasions when you have had to wait for me of an evening. Tonight may be one of them,' Ella conceded, 'but I wouldn't let it worry you.' The tone of voice she used suggested that such concern was the last thing she expected of Rebecca, and Rebecca flushed scarlet.

They were standing half turned away from each other when Oliver joined them. The atmosphere between them could have been cut with a knife.

# Chapter Nineteen

An insensitive man could have detected the alienation between the two women which, from the beginning of the journey had never been too far from the surface. Oliver was far from insensitive but knowing how to deal with the ill-feeling in front of him was quite another matter. He did what most would have done. Nothing. He hovered. Not for long, for Philip was not far behind him. It was long enough. Long enough for Ella to feel abandoned by someone she had been sure was on her side, long enough for Rebecca to lose all sense that Oliver was her protector. In other words it was a disaster.

During the morning they climbed to the Alto de San Roque where once there had been a chapel dedicated to the saint. Now, bestriding the mountain path towards Compostela, was a statue of the saint, staff in hand, pilgrim robes stirred by the wind. 'The patron saint of lepers,' said Jonah.

'Wasn't he a leper himself?' asked Bill.

'I'm not sure. I think I read he was one but was cured in Compostela. Anyway, San Roque went on to complete the pilgrimage to Jerusalem, so he couldn't have been too crippled by the disease. Though he's often pictured with a sore on his leg which is being licked clean by his dog.'

'Yuk,' said Rebecca.

'A very unpleasant disease,' said Bill. 'He must have been a man of great humanity,' he added almost wistfully.

Oliver found himself next to Ella. Each had been thinking privately about their own encounter with Santiago. *Superstitious nonsense – or a mere trick of the light* – was their silent conclusion. Oliver asked solicitously, 'No ill effects from the storm?'

'No. Should there be?'

Her tone was sharp. It was getting to her, this whole thing, the atmosphere of the pilgrimage. He felt bad, too. He should have walked with Ella sooner. He liked her, for God's sake. He admired her guts tremendously, and he enjoyed her company. Santiago would not have approved. 'You are entitled to be feeling a little tired.'

'Oh, for heaven's sake, Oliver, I may be an old woman, but I'm not senile, nor incapacitated, nor am I intending to be a drag on you all. Yes, the storm was unpleasant. No, I wasn't scared out of my wits, such as they are. No, I didn't catch a cold. Yes, I am thoroughly rested. Thank you for your enquiry. Oliver, give me some credit for sense. If I couldn't walk today, I'd have said so. Which your little friend might also have known before she tackled me about it this morning.'

'If you mean Rebecca, she's scarcely my little friend,' he said stiffly. 'I'm sorry if I have said anything to upset you, Ella,' he continued. 'Excuse me.'

For a moment Ella looked thunderous. How dared he take umbrage like that. She had a perfect right to be exactly where she was. Then she grinned to herself. She probably shouldn't have called Rebecca Oliver's 'little friend'. For one thing it was untrue. Rebecca might have been underweight when they started the Camino, she had definitely begun to put on weight recently and really she was quite a solid creature when viewed from the side. Catty, purred Ella to herself. Well, and she was still absolutely furious with Rebecca. And with Oliver for siding quite so obviously with the dratted woman.

Stupid woman, Oliver was thinking crossly. The last thing he had intended was to offend Ella. But what on earth could Rebecca have said to her to have produced that degree of prickliness?

He thought he'd better find out. 'You and Ella have a falling out this morning?' He fell into step beside Rebecca after lunch.

'It's not my fault if she chooses to take offence at a simple enquiry about her health,' Rebecca answered sullenly. Her tone added, *And what is it to you?*

'She is a little sensitive about being thought a drag on us,' he pointed out.

'I know that. I also know that she takes great care not to be one. I still don't think it's exactly sensible for a woman of her age to be on a journey as arduous as this.'

'Come on, Rebecca. You yourself admit she isn't a drag. Personally I find her great company. I'd hate to see her drop out because she felt we were putting the pressure on her to do just that.'

'I certainly haven't done anything to make her feel that way.'

'Not even this morning?' he asked sceptically.

'How dare you. You know, there are times, Oliver, when you are nothing but a bloody prig,' she said furiously. 'If you think I am the sort of person to upset your precious Ella, you'd better go and walk with her. I'd prefer not to be bothered by you.'

'Fine. That's just what I'll do.' He stormed ahead, striding so fast that soon he rounded a bend and was out of sight.

'Oh, damn,' said Rebecca softly, though there was no one within earshot. They'd been getting on so well, she and Oliver. Like real friends. Even. . . . She was beginning to think she could tell him anything and receive a sympathetic hearing, and now look at what had happened.

Oliver felt totally crushed. God, he was so awful about relationships. Once the journey had got under way he'd begun to hope that the enforced proximity would give him a chance to explore ways of delving beneath the surface of people. Like so many others, he had scores of acquaintances but when it came down to it, very few real friends. Life was so superficial nowadays. You never really knew what a person was thinking. Of course, they were all a little strange, those who undertook the Camino, so you could not expect instant bonding of the sort that permitted mutual soul-searching. Individualists they were, all of them. Us, he corrected himself wryly. He could not see himself making a long-term friend of Bill, for example, but he'd like to know how the man ticked. And that did not mean to say he'd never even think of Bill after it was all over. Sharing what they had all experienced, and might still go through, gave them a lot in common. Philip was all right, too, once you got to know him. Deeper than you might suppose at first. Then there was Rebecca. He'd begun to feel quite differently towards her since the mugging. As a friend, naturally, it was not a sexual thing. Once sex entered into a relationship, that always doomed it, in his experience. Then, it certainly did not appear there was anything going for him in any way as far as Rebecca was concerned, though there had been moments when he'd believed they were becoming true friends. Even. . . . Not now.

But Ella was different. He had not thought there would come a time when they would fall out. He'd hated it when she snapped at him like that.

Oliver slowed down: decided he needed a tree. After he had relieved himself he sat down and munched a piece of chocolate. Ah, hell, he thought, he was plainly one of those people who were totally incapable of sustaining any relationship of any significance. He'd better just get used to it.

He returned to the track to find Jonah just behind him. 'Hello,' he said, surprised by finding him there.

'Hi,' Jonah said. 'I thought you were miles ahead.'

'I was. I needed a tree and as usual our speed of walking is really not so different. So you caught me up.'

'I just like the pace as it comes.'

'But you're very good about walking with Ella.'

Jonah shrugged. 'I do that because she's good value.'

'I'm glad you appreciate her.'

'We all do, in our own way, even Bill. We all seem to be changing our perspectives as the days go by. Haven't you noticed?'

'Bill is certainly far less touchy. One might say. . . .'

'Almost human? But Ella has become very defensive.'

'I know. We're probably all to blame there. Especially me. Currently she's furious with me.' He told Jonah what had happened that morning.

'If Ella is furious, it's probably a robust sign. I wouldn't worry. All you have to do is say sorry.'

'You make relationships sound very easy,' Oliver said. 'I wish. . . .'

'Don't be a prat,' Jonah said. 'There isn't a relationship that doesn't have its bad patches. If it means anything to you, you just have to do something to mend it.'

Oliver digested the advice. Strangely he felt no animosity that it should come from someone so much younger. 'Has Rebecca changed?' he asked eventually.

Jonah snorted in derision. 'Of all the leading questions. You don't have to ask me mate, though judging from that little row you had this morning, I guess there are a few fences that need mending there.'

'You heard us?'

'I think we all heard the end of it.'

'It wasn't – isn't a laughing matter.'

'Sorry. None of my business. I like Rebecca. I think she has integrity. I'd hate to see her hurt.'

'I don't like hurting anyone,' Oliver said hastily, refusing the bait held out to him. Somehow it seemed disloyal to continue discussing either Ella or Rebecca with anyone else. 'Thanks, ' he said eventually. 'I suspect I was being a bit of a prig,' he added, unconsciously echoing Rebecca's accusation of that morning. 'I guess I'll just have to do a bit of grovelling.'

'Probably doesn't do any harm to grovel occasionally, as long as you don't overdo it.'

He shot Jonah a startled look. It was extraordinary how the boy came out with the most perspicacious comments. 'Or else become a hermit,' he murmured. Jonah was still chortling as they caught up with Bill.

'Someone sounds cheerful,' Bill turned to greet them. 'Oh, it's you.'

Jonah chose not to take offence. 'Oliver thinks he might become a hermit. Now, I ask you, why, with a gorgeous redhead just ready and waiting?' And shaking his head, he walked on to catch up with Philip.

'Silly youth,' said Bill morosely. 'So flippant.'

'Scarcely that.'

'Facile, then.'

'Not in the least,' Oliver found himself defending Jonah roundly. 'He has a strong sense of the righteous, if you ask me.'

And with that he, too, quickened his pace.

On the outskirts of Triacastela Jonah told them to pick up a stone. 'We must carry this to Castañeda,' he said. 'The stones are for the furnaces where the lime was prepared for the building of the cathedral at Santiago.'

'Not in use now, are they?' asked Rebecca.

'Not a clue. It's tradition.'

'Right,' she said. 'I'll find something small.'

At Samos they visited the great Benedictine monastery. Philip said, 'If you think I am missing out on about the only really interestin' bit of sculpture along the route, you have to be jokin'.'

'You mean the Cloister of the Nereids?' asked Bill.

'Yeah. Naked nymphs, the guidebook says.'

'Bound to be a disappointment,' commented Jonah sagely.

Philip and Ella were standing together in front of yet another sculptured Descent into Hell, explicitly gruesome in its gory detail of the punishments awaiting the wicked in the life to come. 'Gettin' the teeniest bit bored with this theme,' observed Philip, shaking his head over a particularly inventive, not to say sadistic devil. 'What do you think about it all?'

'If you mean the entire Spanish architectural thing we've been seeing, I've found it fascinating,' replied Ella.

'You don't mean to say you actually like it?'

'Not like it, exactly,' she said cautiously. 'In fact, I think that if I were to be faced with it every Sunday for the rest of my life, I would be appalled. But, then that's what it was all about, isn't it?'

'You mean the church was literally putting the fear of God into its followers.'

'Of course. And considering the level of literacy at that time, a piece of sculpture, a mural, anything graphic was bound to have an impact.'

'Particularly when allied to scriptural readings? Yes, I see that. Maybe we should have a lot more of it in the modern church, given what they say about the attention span of yoof.'

Ella laughed. 'Yet when you consider the hardships suffered by the pilgrims then, there must have been a good few who really wanted to give up the pilgrimage only to be brought back into line by something like this, the fear of what might happen after a person died.'

'You do like it.'

'As an art form, I admire it. I don't like it.'

'So it tells us what they thought about the afterlife centuries ago. What does it do for us nowadays, Ella?'

Ella smiled ruefully. 'I'm sure I don't know. I mean, I doubt if more than a minute proportion of modern pilgrims actually believes in hot pincers, boiling oil, or whatever it is, hell, even. As for your average Sunday churchgoer, your guess is as good as mine.'

Philip put his head on one side as he examined the piece further. He was silent for some moments. 'Do you believe in an afterlife, Ella?' he asked. 'If that isn't a frightfully impertinent question.'

Ella sighed. 'I'm afraid I have a reputation at home for being an outspoken critic of everything contentious in the Church. I certainly came away with basic Christian beliefs intact, if that is any sort of an answer. Now? Actually I'm finding all this rather difficult,' she confessed.

'Talking to me about it? I say, I'm dreadfully sorry. If. . . .'

'No. Please excuse me, Philip. That's not what I meant at all. You see, I don't think you can get this far on an undertaking such as ours without changing in some way.'

'Right,' he agreed. 'I'll go along with that.'

'I also don't see how anyone can logically deny the existence of God – when you see the mountains, the scenery, go into the truly magnificent churches we've visited.'

'You mean that a graphically illustrated scene from hell proves the existence of the place? Not sure I quite go along with the logic of that,' he remarked.

Ella looked startled. 'Ah, I may not have explained myself as well as I wanted to. What I meant to say is that I believe in God and in the existence of the soul, but I'm not too sure about the intervention of the churches – of whatever denomination.' She sighed again. 'I think I may find it difficult to attend church with quite the frequency I used to without considering myself ever so slightly hypocritical.'

'That's interestin',' said Philip. 'Very interesting. In fact my own case is almost the opposite.'

'Don't tell me you've found religion,' said Ella sharply. 'Oh, I apologize again, Philip. That was also unpardonable.'

Philip smiled. 'And totally inaccurate. No. In the past, I've gone to church regularly but I confess it was really only because it was there. You know, rising accountant wants to be seen to be doing the right thing. I've even done a stint as churchwarden. Now that must shock you.'

'Not at all,' said Ella. 'I know very well just how difficult it is to find someone not only willing but capable of doing that job. I think there's many a parish priest who has thanked the Lord for small mercies and not inquired too closely into the private beliefs of his PCC, especially anyone with a job that depends on reliability. But things are different now?' she suggested, after a pause.

'I don't know. Possibly. I think when I return home I shall have to do some reading round the subject. Yes, I guess you are probably right, though just how much I've changed with regard to the church remains to be seen. And what Posy will think about it, I really don't know.'

'Why does she come into the equation?'

'No idea. Now that's a novel thought.'

'You don't think Posy has undergone her own change, just by not having you around?'

Philip shook his head. 'Can't say I've found any difference when we've been talking over the phone,' he admitted. And was that true? And if she had changed, what was that going to do with their relationship when he returned? That was a thought, indeed.

# Chapter Twenty

No one asked Bill about the state of his soul, or if he had one, or even if there was a possibility that he possessed no such thing. The rest of the group was perfectly at ease asking Bill about the mundane details of the walk – how far to the next refuge, did they need to ring ahead to a hostel and book? Were they going to find a decent meal at the end of the day? Philip might consult Ella; Oliver would, almost, bare his soul to Rebecca, until that little spat they'd had so publicly. No one would have dreamt of touching on the strictly personal with Bill. Which, when you consider his calling, the pastoral work he had been doing for the past umpteen years, was somewhat strange, even though no one knew he was a priest.

Bill was not cut out to be a Samaritan. He was actually a little contemptuous of people's frailties. He could not understand addiction. Habit, yes; he walked in the hills habitually, but it was a pastime he could abandon without it causing him the slightest angst. Alcohol, drugs, the sort of sex that went on in under-the-counter magazines or videos, those vices appalled him. He pitied the people who were in thrall to them, but he was never quite sure what to say to them that would make the least difference to their lives, or the lives of the others most close to them or affected by them. Which, he was slowly and painfully beginning to understand, did not make him a particularly successful pastor, bums on seats being beside the point. Which was all very difficult, given his circumstances. It was true to say that up to now the pilgrimage, far from resolving Bill's problems, had resulted in worse feelings of turmoil, uncertainty, doubt and perplexity.

Had anyone asked Bill about his soul, the answer would have been that he most certainly possessed one, but its state was purely a matter between himself and the Lord. As for where he stood with the church. . . . It is more than likely that Bill would have frozen his inquisitor with a look long before the entire question might be framed.

Portomarín was now a modern village which they approached along a new bridge over the River Miño and across the reservoir under which the old village was submerged, climbing the newly-positioned ancient and steep steps to the Chapel of the Virgen de las Nieves before visiting the reconstructed Church of San Nicolas, the numbers still visible on some of its stones which had been painted on as the building was being taken down.

'Electric candles,' grumbled Ella. 'I suppose it's too much to expect something as old-fashioned as proper candles here. Pity. It was a good walk today. I'd have liked something to light.'

They all opted for the large, traditional hostel and in the morning persuaded the parish priest to stamp their pilgrim passports.

They were queuing for the stamp. Bill was bending over the table at which the priest sat. Philip was waiting at the end of the line, not really thinking of anything in particular, when suddenly his memory clicked into focus. *No, surely not* . . . was his first thought. He put his head on one side and began to think. It was not his habit to peruse minutely the endless columns devoted to the peccadilloes of the human race even in the broadsheets. He actively disliked the prurience with which each occurrence was revealed daily, but there had been one, relating to the marital problems of a vicar, which had interested Posy inordinately. She waxed lyrical in her defence of the wife – inevitably Philip had felt drawn to support the betrayed husband. *Put a dog collar on the man, and he was the spittin' image of Bill.* Well, well, thought Philip. If he was right, and he was positive he was, that actually explained a lot about the man.

He thought he would mention his suspicions to Posy. If it really were Bill, the man had a perfect right to the anonymity he so plainly craved, but seeking confirmation from an outside source was different. It was not as if he would blurt out the truth to the rest. Not for one moment, so far as Philip knew, had Bill given the slightest indication that he was ordained. Well, he'd think about it. He'd mull it over and maybe tell her when they next spoke.

They had decided not to spend a day at Portomarín. 'We have to do the detour to Vilar de Donas,' Bill said. 'The guidebook says it's the most outstanding small Romanesque church in the area so I suggest we do that together out of Palas de Rei on our day off.'

'How about it, Ella?' asked Oliver. 'Can you manage the extra day?'

Ella had been studying the map. She said, 'I guess I'll go along with that. We might even find a taxi around the N 540 if the going seems a bit rough.'

'Not very likely,' he said dubiously. 'They are very small hamlets we pass through.'

'Oh, there's bound to be something in Palas de Rei.'

But by lunch time they had not seen anything that might turn out to be transport. It was a straggling line that forgathered for a break. 'Hey, what is it with you lot today?' Jonah asked them all. 'Can't get more than a syllable out of any of you.'

Oliver shrugged. Rebecca looked away. Ella muttered, 'I'm tired, dear boy.' The others said nothing.

Jonah said, 'OK. OK. I guess I've missed the ripples. Doesn't matter.'

'Perhaps it was a bad idea, missing out on the rest day. Sorry Ella,' said Bill.

'It isn't that,' said Rebecca surprisingly. 'I think we've just become aware that we are not so very far off Santiago de Compostela. That's probably what's making us a bit subdued.' Even why we are arguing, she thought to herself. 'Got any good stories to relieve the tedium, Jonah?'

'Not really. There's a bit in the book about harlots going out to meet pilgrims in wild parts between Portomarín and Palas de Rei. That's about all.'

'You're jokin',' commented Philip. 'Here?'

'That's what it says. Also that they '*should not only be excommunicated, but also stripped of everything and exposed to public ridicule, after having their noses cut off.*'

'Charming,' murmured Rebecca.

'They were a bit more robust in their thinking in those days,' said Bill.

'What days?' asked Ella.

'It's in the *Liber Sancti Jacobi*,' said Jonah.

'Herbers,' said Bill. 'Middle of the eighteenth century.'

'Exactly.'

Philip observed the exchange, a sardonic expression on his face.

Posy had returned home and that evening he was on the phone to her. 'Cast your mind back some months. I think I have a mystery for you to solve. Something I think I know about Bill.'

'So, tell me?' He did. 'I don't believe you.'

'Suit yourself. I think you'll find I'm right and Bill is the vicar who chased his wife and her lover through their garden brandishing a huge whip.'

'You amaze me,' she said. 'And even if you are correct, which I doubt, you have no right to spread the story round people he must have come to believe are his friends.'

'I haven't spread the story,' he protested. 'I'm just mentioning it to you. Actually, considering how at the time I blamed the wife, I think maybe you could have been right in blaming the husband.'

'Oh, yes,' she answered suspiciously. 'How do you make that out?'

'Maybe he's one of those queers there seem to be so many of in the church.'

Over the miles that separated them, Philip could see her shaking her head. 'First you come out with a far-fetched notion that Bill is an unfrocked priest—'

'I never said that,' he interrupted. 'You must remember how he seemed to dislike our Jonah intensely at first. Now they're really pally.'

'So perhaps Bill has realized that there is a lot of good in Jonah. You certainly seem to have changed your tune about the boy. Philip, I hope you're not going to say any of this to anyone else?'

'No,' though he didn't sound too sure.

'It's a theory. Nothing else. If you like, I'll do some researching, but if you ask me, I think you've been thinking far too hard on this walk. Making two and two equal even more than five. You want to keep your friends, I think you should be very careful what you go around saying.'

'Or perhaps I haven't been thinking quite hard enough,' he said slowly. Ella was right, he was thinking. Posy had changed. She'd become harder. No, maybe that was not it. She'd definitely become more positive in her attitudes. She never used to challenge him quite like this in the old days, first over the house, then where she went while he was away. In the old days she'd been happy enough to go along with whatever he suggested. Then, maybe not only did he have to do a lot more thinking, they had to do a lot of talking. He had a strange feeling that the world – his world – had shifted just when he least expected it. It was unsettling.

He had also begun by making these frequent calls to his wife as a matter of duty. At first, having to bring his mind back to her and the family had been a considerable effort. Recently, somewhat to his surprise, he had discovered that not only did he enjoy telling her about the journey and hearing what she was doing, he was really looking forward to seeing her again. After a pause which he realized had gone on for too long, 'How would it be if you came to Santiago to meet me?' he suggested eagerly. 'We might even stay on for a few days. I could do with a bit of a holiday before I pick up the threads at home again. What do you say?'

'Well,' Posy began, 'I had promised to look after the girls. . . .' Had she, too, begun to wonder how it would be after this time of separation? His heart missed a beat as he waited for her answer. 'Why not? I think that's a lovely idea. We've got such a lot to talk about. I'll see if I can get a cheap ticket.'

'Don't worry too much about the cost, dear. Just come.'

'Philip, about Bill. I don't need to ferret. You are right. I remember, and it was tabloid-messy. He caught his wife in bed with the local butcher and chased them both stark naked from the house. The lover escaped but left the wife to find refuge with neighbours. I don't know what happened next but Bill Dyson was given extensive leave-of-absence from his parish.'

'Fascinating.'

'Philip, you won't say anything, will you?' Posy's concern was clear over the distance separating them.

'Mm? Probably not.'

'No. You mustn't, please. It might have been common knowledge then, it would be very unfair to rehash something that I bet he hates to remember.'

'You're right, of course,' Philip agreed reluctantly. 'Still, it's nice to know the old memory hasn't completely gone to pot.'

'I never supposed that it had. So, thanks for calling, and I'll see you very soon.'

Vilar de Donas was worth the detour. Founded in the tenth century as a nunnery, it was taken over in 1184 by the Knights of the Order of St James to become its official burial place in Galicia. To the nunnery, it was believed, had repaired widows of Crusader knights to live out their days in comfort. The walls were covered with frescos: an Annunciation and what were said to be portraits of the 'donas', in the head-dresses of their period, some of them very beautiful women.

Rebecca was sure there was also a green man depicted in a pale red wash on the west wall, though Ella disagreed. 'How can you say those leaves are actually coming from that mouth?'

'It seems plain enough to me. Look how the mouth seems to widen at the edges to accommodate the stalk.'

Privately thinking that it looked more like a puff of wind than a stalk, Ella, mindful of her earlier belief that they were all niggling at each other only through exhaustion, thanked

Rebecca for pointing it out. Mollified, Rebecca offered Ella a eucalyptus sweet on the way back to the hotel.

Philip sat on soft grass in dappled shade with his back propped against a rock. He was totally alone, an event for which he was profoundly grateful for it happened so seldom. Once he got home he would make time for himself, he resolved, time to read, time to reflect. He knew it would not be achieved without effort but he was determined that it must be done. There were many things to discuss with Posy and now, at last, he realized that changes he might relish might not be to her liking – or changes she would like might not be to his taste. Somehow, though, he had no doubts that they would accommodate each other.

He had with him his exercise book which was now three-quarters full of scribbling. There were notes on scenery, incidents that had occurred on the Camino that had interested him. There were even jottings of meals that he had particularly liked. Those meals, incidentally, were getting to him a little. Most nights recently he'd had a spot of indigestion. He'd go to bed thoroughly exhausted and fall asleep immediately only to wake around three feeling extremely uncomfortable, fidgety, bloated. He only hoped his antacid tablets would last out because he was getting through them at quite a rate. Not that they seemed to be doing him all that good, either. Once he got home he'd definitely need to go on a diet. He thought that he'd not put on all that weight because of the walking. Still, a little less intake, of everything, probably would not come amiss.

Starting from the back of his exercise book was his poetry – admittedly most of it crossed out, though a few, a very few thoughts and lines were underscored as possessing a little merit. Philip had long ago abandoned rhyme (it was far too difficult composing couplets that were not utterly banal). Now he was almost coming to the end of something that pleased him. Obviously it needed polishing and he would probably leave that until they had returned home, but on the whole he did not think it was too bad at all.

Across the years Santiago called
And pilgrims listened and came.
They tramped high mountain passes,
The inexorable plain,
Arched bridges,
Sunken lanes.
Awe-inspiring cathedrals,
Simple chapels, graves
Stirred inchoate senses.
Though too much Hell for a sinner such as he.
Was it for this he'd drawn near,
His soul's salvation?

The sentiment said what he wanted to say. He wished his vocabulary were larger – he'd dredged 'inchoate' from somewhere, which was rather good (but wished he had a dictionary to check the usage). Yes, it was all right for a beginning. He might even join a poets' group when they got home. They said feedback was a salutary thing. An anthology would be quite something to aim for. Though he might not show anyone this, his very first effort. The sun had moved so that it warmed his lower body. Uneasily he shifted to a more comfortable position, closed his eyes, and dozed.

# Chapter Twenty-One

There were less than sixty kilometres to walk: the end was in sight. Bill, Ella and Jonah were walking together. Ella asked, 'What story are you saving for us today?'

'You tryin' to put one over the rest?'

'Certainly not. I just wondered who figures in it today, that's all.'

Jonah shrugged. 'Actually I don't think I have one.'

'Goodness me. You can't fail us now, young man.'

'The river we've just crossed,' said Bill, 'it's the Ruxian. That means River Julian in these parts. I think it refers to St Julian who has historical links with pilgrims.'

'Tenuous links,' argued Jonah, 'all legend, anyway.'

'St Julian. That's all I want to know,' said Ella. 'You can tell us the rest later.'

'Hardly worth botherin',' muttered Jonah to her back, kicking a stone out of his way.

'You can't disappoint them now,' protested Bill. 'You know they usually want a story or something when we regroup.'

'So I always have to indulge them?' he said sullenly.

Bill stopped. 'What's the matter?'

Jonah shrugged again.

Bill persisted, 'Don't you feel well, or something?'

'What's it to you?'

'Nothing, absolutely nothing,' Bill began angrily, 'if. . . .' He stopped. It was happening again – he was doing it again, failing to communicate. 'That's not true. You've been good – company – these last weeks. If there is anything the matter, I'd like to help.'

'Streuth.' Jonah saw the glint of outrage in the older man's eyes. He held up his hand in apology. 'I guess I'm just not sure what happens when we get to Santiago, that's all.'

'You'll get your Compostela, if that's what you mean.'

'It wasn't.'

'No. Money problems?'

Jonah grunted a denial. 'That's the last thing on my mind.'

'Then what. . . .'

'I just wonder what you'll all do then.'

'What we do? That's a peculiar statement for a young man to make.'

'Don't be so fuckin' patronizing.'

Choosing not to take offence, Bill said patiently, 'I meant, why should it matter to you what we do?'

'I guess I feel responsible, in a way. If I hadn't joined up with you, would you all have stayed together?'

'Of course we would.' Bill's answer was instant. He saw a quizzical look cross Jonah's face. Would they have stayed together? How many of them would have stayed together? 'That is, I don't know. What do you think?'

Appealed to, Jonah seemed to relax. 'I guess Philip would still be walking with us. Rebecca and Oliver would too.'

'Why do you lump those two together? I was under the impression they disliked each other intensely.'

'You're jokin'. Thick as two thieves they are. Oh, I know they've had their rows, but can't you feel the attraction between them?'

'I can only sense tension.'

Jonah grinned. 'Same thing, man.'

Bill did his best not to appear irritated. 'Ella would have given up by now without you,' he said instead, giving credit where credit was due. 'It's a long way, for a woman of that age, on her own.'

'She might have gone to Santiago by bus or train and be there already.'

'Or have found someone nearer her own age and be somewhere behind us,' said Bill shrewdly. 'And where am I in all this?' he asked, not without humour.

'Ah. There's a question. I tell you where you will be, though, if we continue gassing in one spot like this?'

'And where is that?'

'They'll be thinkin' that you've seen the light and are chattin' me up.'

'What are you talk. . . . Are you suggesting. . . ?' When Jonah merely grinned at him, Bill continued, 'How dare you suggest. . . . I've never heard. . . . What utter rubbish. . . .' He turned so apoplectic with fury that for a moment Jonah wondered if he'd have a fit. Then he turned on his heel and strode off.

Jonah caught up with him. He said gently, 'It's rubbish about me. I'm not gay. I wouldn't really know about you.'

Bill stopped abruptly. He was deathly white. 'Is that what you think of me? That I'm a homosexual? That's horrible, disgusting.'

'Common practice in many parts of the world.'

'Not where I come from.'

'So it worries you that I suggest it might be a possibility?'

'Of course it does. I'm a married. . . .'

'I thought you might have been. Once.'

'I still am. Legally.'

'Look,' said Jonah, 'I don't really want to know what your sexual orientation is. I told you, I'm just interested to know what you are going to do once we reach Santiago. Goin' back to your wife, then, are you?'

'I – I – I. . . . No. I don't think so.'

'There, that wasn't so hard to say, after all, was it?'

'Who are you to question me like this? How dare you?' Bill repeated angrily, turning on Jonah, standing in the middle of the path his sticks in one hand, his other arm flapping as if all he wanted was to make violent contact with it.

'Easy, mate. I'm just a friend. That's all. You know, I've tried picturing you in various roles – businessman, social worker, whatever. Without success. Guess you're just a bit of a mystery.'

With visible effort Bill allowed his aggression to subside. There was a rock by the side of the path. He slumped against it.

Eyes narrowed, alert for another outburst, Jonah went on,

'Except, you know, I've always seen you in some vaulted cloister. Like the ones we've been in along the Camino. Walking along to prayer with a string of other monks in the dead of night with your cowl half-obscuring your face.'

'To matins, I expect,' said Bill drily. He examined his hands. They were shaking slightly. 'If the cowl was half-obscuring my face, how did you know it was me?'

'How indeed. You ever wear a dog collar?'

'I might have.'

'Thought so. Not that it's any of my business. Think Philip might have cottoned on to it, though.'

'No, it isn't any of your business,' hissed Bill angrily.

'But you might thank me for the warning. Oh, look, they're waiting for us.'

'St Julian,' called Ella.

'No. I'm Jonah, not Julian. And I may have disappointed them, I didn't kill my parents.'

'Kill your parents?'

'Whatever is the boy talking about now?' asked Oliver, emerging from behind a boulder.

'St Julian was a nobleman who killed his parents accidentally.'

'A likely story,' Ella said suspiciously.

'The legend goes that one day he was out hunting a stag,' said Jonah, squatting beside Ella. He seemed to have forgotten he'd not thought the story worth telling. 'His prey turned on him reproachfully and warned him that one day he'd kill his parents.'

'A talking beast,' said Ella jubilantly. 'Sorry,' she said penitently, 'go on.'

'Julian fled from home, taking service with the king of another country who knighted him and married him to a rich widow, called Adela, who brought with her a castle as dowry. Some years later his parents, who had never ceased to search for him, arrived at the castle. Adela gave them her own room. Julian returned while she was at church. Seeing a man and a woman in Adela's bed, Julian jumped to the not unnatural conclusion his wife'd taken a lover, so he killed them both.

When he discovered what had happened, Julian and Adela left the castle and became wanderers. So to expurgate his sin, Julian founded a hospice for pilgrims which he ran with Adela. Then, one day a leper came and Julian gave him his own bed. The leper died but Julian had a vision of the leper's departing soul and from this he deduced he'd won divine pardon. Don't know what happened after that,' he finished airily.

'You do talk a load of nonsense at times,' said Bill, as he so often did. This time he said it without conviction. Take himself. He'd acted quite legitimately, striking out at his wife and her lover, and look at where that had brought him.

Philip said shrewdly. 'They're all very moral stories, though, aren't they? You know, man finds wife *in flagrante delicto*, wants to kill her, discovers he's got the wrong woman after all, has to make reparation—'

'Yes, yes,' said Bill hurriedly. 'Wanting instant revenge may not be a very worthy sentiment, but it's – it must be very satisfying.'

'It's very human,' said Ella, and her eyes were warm with understanding.

'I guess it's worth dinner, anyway,' said Oliver, oblivious to the nuances.

'But isn't it marvellous how it's always the women in Jonah's tales who are either the scapegoats or who suffer, or both, in these legends,' said Rebecca sarcastically.

Bill opened his mouth as though to expostulate. Then he closed it.

Ella said, 'I don't think it's the tales Jonah chooses. I think it's the times they depict.'

'And that's supposed to make me feel better?' Rebecca went pink, waited for Ella to demur. Ella merely laughed and the moment passed.

When they walked on, Bill found himself next to Ella. This, as they both knew, was unusual. They walked near each other, sometimes, but always separated by one or other of the group. He saw a gap opening between Rebecca and Jonah and began to move off, but it was closed by Philip. One person he did not want to walk with was Philip. Under the circumstances.

Ella opened the conversation. 'What were you going to say, back there?'

'Say? I wasn't going to say anything.'

'I beg your pardon. I had a different impression. It seemed as though you were going to say something about Jonah. He doesn't really sponge off us, you know. He gives us as much as we give him.'

'And how do you work that out?' he asked.

'Most of us thoroughly enjoy his stories, and look how we all rely on him whenever we need good Spanish.'

Bill seemed to sag. 'You're the second person to tell me today that I'm never right about anything.'

'Of course you're right, sometimes.'

'Jonah was wrong about me.' His voice rose in indignation. He could keep silent about that insinuation no longer. 'He's just accused me of being a – a gay.' It burst from him as though he could not keep it to himself, no matter whom he told.

'Such a misnomer, I always feel, gay. But you're not.'

'No. At least, I'm fairly sure I'm not. I mean, I've never had any – any sexual feelings about other men. To be perfectly honest I'm more comfortable talking to men but as for the other. . . .'

'I know.'

'How do you know . . . what do you know?' Hostility in his voice, Bill turned towards Ella to find her gazing at him with deep compassion. 'I'm a married man,' he insisted as if he were waiting for her to accuse him of the unmentionable.

'I thought an unhappy marriage might be the problem.'

Bill sighed. 'Legally I'm still married,' he said, as he had told Jonah. 'I'm considering whether or not to go back to her.'

'Does she get a say in this getting back together scenario?'

'Well I . . . well. It probably won't happen,' he admitted. 'Even if she . . . I'm not sure that I. . . .' He sighed, seemed to sag under the backpack. 'I was I . . . am . . . a parish priest. My wife committed adultery and there was a somewhat public washing of dirty linen over it.'

'Ah. I had wondered. I seem to remember something about it.'

'Have you. . . ?'

'Told anyone. Certainly not, though I really couldn't say if the others suspect.'

'I have the feeling Philip may know.'

'I can assure you I won't mention it, and I don't think Philip would, either. What are you going to do? Will you go back to your parish?'

'I don't know. I thought the Camino would give me the answers. All it seems to have done is ask questions.'

Ella smiled. 'And provide uncomfortable thoughts about all sorts of things.' She did not elaborate.

Bill was too preoccupied by his own problems to wonder what in Ella's life needed considering. 'A hermit,' he said wistfully. 'It would be good to leave the world, live in a cave or a hut in the woods or on the top of a pole. Do you remember learning about Simon Stylites? He's the one who lived on the top of a pole for thirty-seven years and whose disciples visited him regularly with what food he needed.'

'I've always thought that was a less than admirable way of going about gaining righteousness. Wasn't there a song, or something about, "*Stop the world, I want to get off!*" I sometimes get that feeling when I'm tired but underneath I know it's not possible and I've just got to get on with things.'

'I suppose actually being a hermit is a tremendous discipline,' Bill said. 'Jonah told me this morning he saw me in a monk's cowl.'

'Did he now? I've always thought that young man has hidden depths.'

'Well,' said Bill uncomfortably, 'whatever, I – I'm. . . .'

'Sort of floundering. You won't be, when we get to Santiago.'

'I wish I could be so sure.'

There not being any obvious sign of a working furnace in Castañeda, they left their limestones at the parish church.

It was their last day but one. Way out in front, Bill was walking with his lungs fully open, breathing freely, striding with an effortless pace, for once at ease with the world – at least with the few people who currently made up his world. Curiously, in the night, certain decisions seemed to have been made without his volition. He'd not go back to Mary, always assuming she wanted him, he admitted with rare humility, which seemed unlikely. The marriage was over. It probably should never have taken place. But it had. And for their peace of mind in the future they had to live apart. Yet the marriage had left a problem, caused a human problem in the shape of their daughter, Elspeth. With a sense of appalled shame, Bill wondered how it was he could have produced a daughter and then had such little thought about her, either in the past once she was comfortably out of his sight at her school, or more recently when he had been agonizing over his own future. That surely made him a failure twice over – as a father and as a human being? His inability to be a good husband to Mary was one thing; his failure to be a father to Elspeth was quite another. Could that be put right? He sighed heavily, the fragile peace of mind with which he had started the day threatened by affairs which were certainly not going to be put right by a simple apology or even a short conversation. But it was something he had to do.

Then there was his work. He could neither go back to his parish, nor seek another. Not now, the calling was not for him. But neither could he abandon the life of the church. He had no idea whether he was a homosexual or not. What he had told Ella was the truth – that he was infinitely more at ease in the presence of men than he was with women. If that made him a homosexual then perhaps he was. The whole confused business of sex bewildered him so much that he could see the attraction of celibacy. As a hermit? There were still hermits in parts of the world today. Find a cosy cave. It had its attractions. Maybe that was the answer. He smiled at the thought of living at the top of a pole. But Simon Stylites must have been an uncomfortable sort of chap. Even for those times when such behaviour was regarded merely as one man's way to God. No, Ella was right about hermits. The world, his world, was too populated to have room for hermits. But celibacy for the remainder of his days . . . the life of a monk. . . . Now that might well be his for if there was one lesson the Camino had taught him it was the power of prayer. His bishop had sent him for counselling after the episode with Mary and her lover. It was Father Jerome who had suggested the Camino. He'd talk to Father Jerome, when they got home. And maybe this time there'd be fewer negative feelings to work through.

# Chapter Twenty-Two

Time was getting short for making up.

There was that in Bill's demeanour as he passed him that warned Oliver not to match his stride. Yet it was not the pace of a man whose demons were chasing him; rather a man, if not entirely at peace, at least coming to terms with himself. 'Lucky for some,' thought Oliver gloomily, recalling the frosty glare that had been his only thanks from Rebecca for a mint sweet, the short 'Good morning' that was all Ella had to offer as they met up after breakfast. Perhaps it was his mission today to mend fences. Or at least try to.

Ella was at the back. He sat on a boulder and waited for her to catch up then he fell into step beside her. 'One more day to go,' he said. 'It's strange to think that tomorrow we arrive in Santiago.'

'I have yet to decide whether I can do this final long stretch,' she replied. 'I thought I might pick up transport in Arzúa and meet you in Arca.'

'Aches and pains?'

'No, just *Anno Domini*.'

'You've done fantastically well.'

'Considering my age?'

'Considering nothing. They can hardly refuse you your Compostela for a bit of four-wheeled help.'

'I'm not sure whether I shall ask for the Compostela.'

'Really? I thought most of us came with that very intention.'

'Most of us?'

'I don't think Rebecca ever wanted it.'

'I'm sorry we quarrelled over Rebecca,' Ella said abruptly. 'Should know better at my age than to take offence over trifles.'

'We're exhausted and overwhelmed by what we've already achieved so that's why we bicker?'

'I'm sure that's right. Personally I don't think I ever really thought I'd get here. I think it was always in the back of my mind that I'd fall so far behind that I'd have to opt out, take the train or something. I always thought I'd reach Santiago, just not with the people I started out with. A lot of that is thanks to you, Oliver.'

'And Jonah,' he said unexpectedly.

She smiled. 'Yes, and Jonah. I wonder what that young man will do when we separate.'

'Go and annoy someone else, I shouldn't wonder.'

'I hope he makes it up with his mother.'

'His mother. Have you got that right, Ella? I had the distinct impression that it was Jonah's father who had left him and his mother.'

'That's very peculiar. When we were still speaking, Rebecca told me that she was sure Jonah had told her he was orphaned at an early age. I just thought she'd misunderstood. I never bothered to check.'

They looked at each other and a glimmer of dawning comprehension lit Oliver's eyes. 'I think our Jonah has great histrionic talent. I've often wondered if he intends to become an actor but I don't suppose we shall ever know the truth about that young man. My guess is he's just running away from everything, after all, like the rest of us.'

'Are you still running away, Oliver?' she asked softly.

He shrugged. 'Probably. I only know I'm still a mess of don't knows, if you see what I mean. What will you do, Ella? Once we get to Santiago.'

'Have a few days there. Relax a bit. Fly home. The usual.'

'Then what?' he persisted.

'Interrogation time?' she asked.

'I'm interested. I get the feeling that none of us is going home quite as we set out.'

'That's certainly true. All right. Confession time. When I get home I'm going to sell my house. It's far too big and I'm getting too old to make the garden pay. I shall buy something very small – with a tiny garden because I couldn't bear to be without growing things – and invest the rest. Then I shall save up to go travelling.'

'Travelling.'

'Now, that does surprise you,' she said complacently.

'A bit. What sort of travelling?'

'Long distance, cheaply. I know how to cope with that now so it wouldn't scare me and there are all sorts of places I'd like to see. Rome, parts of the Middle East, India.'

'I had a conversation very like this with Rebecca,' he said, 'when we were having conversations. I never saw you as the type to sit at the feet of a guru. A few weeks ago I think you might have sounded off about spiritual tourism if one of us had even suggested that sort of travelling.'

'Oh dear, what a dreadful old bag you must have thought me. Spiritual tourism? Is that what it'd be?'

'Probably not. It's not like the supported groups who do the Camino.'

'You know, if I ever did sneer at that, I wouldn't now,' Ella said, 'and maybe not anyway at spiritual tourism, though truly, I don't think I am the sort who seeks out gurus. But what you get out of a pilgrimage is what you put into it, don't you think?'

'That's wise.'

'I doubt it. Maybe just old age and aching bones. One more day, huh? Goodness, I suppose we will all make it, then.'

In the end, Ella walked the whole way that last-but-one day, and as they passed through a eucalyptus wood she was pleased she had changed her mind. She snapped off a small stem to take home and put several leaves in her pocket which she took out occasionally to sniff, the strong scent of the crushed foliage clearing her lungs and making it easier to walk. The Camino skirts the little village of Arca, but there was a small hotel with a good restaurant on the main road through the village to which they diverted, promising Jonah a last night at their expense. They were elated, yet subdued at the same time. Just a few more kilometres before journey's end.

*

They had come to the river at Lavacolla – scarcely more than a stream. Jonah said, 'This is where traditionally pilgrims stripped off their clothes and washed their bodies, paying particular attention to their private parts.'

'Goodness,' exclaimed Ella. 'I trust this is not mandatory.'

'Everybody did it. They washed and changed their clothing which I expect was highly desirable after all that travelling. All the same, it was obviously ritualistic,' said Bill. 'Picaud's *Pilgrims' Guide* says they do it in a leafy spot for the love of the Apostle and it's about two miles from the outskirts of Compostela from here.'

'Just by the airport,' murmured Philip reflectively, wondering if Posy had already arrived, easing his left shoulder under the strap of his backpack which seemed heavier than ever. Rhythmically he rubbed his upper arm which had developed a dull ache. He was also feeling slightly nauseous. He hoped he wasn't coming down with something. It would be a pity to spoil their few days' holiday.

'The water's cold,' said Rebecca who had dipped a finger in, 'even at the end of summer.'

Ella knelt down beside her, leant over and scooped a handful with which she dabbed her face. 'Ritual completed,' she said.

The others, good-humouredly, did much the same, but Philip had removed his backpack and was now stepping gingerly from one uneven stone to another. He reached the middle of the stream where he stood for a moment balancing precariously. The prospect of cool water cascading deliciously over his head was alluring. 'Might as well do it properly,' he said clearly and bent forward.

They were ribbing him. 'Good old Philip.'

'Just as well one of us is prepared to do the right thing.'

'Get your clothes off, then.'

The water was so cold it took his breath away. He gasped, and it was no better and a band of something began to fasten itself round his chest and tighten and tighten. He opened his mouth to object to what was happening but there was no breath to breathe. He flailed his hands, one grasping his collar to loosen it at the neck for air, precious air, the other groping above the stream as if trying to scoop up more of the water for simple relief.

They were still laughing as he toppled forward. At first it seemed he was playing the clown, had done it on purpose for a jest. But Philip did not move from where he had fallen. He lay in the stream motionless, legs splayed, one boot totally submerged, one hand trailing over the edge of a rock, his head dangling out of sight away from them. As Philip's world grew dark, it was the water that filled his mind. Clean water, blessed water. The stuff of life. His soul's salvation. . . .

It was the submerged boot that alerted Bill. The one thing a walker does not do deliberately is to soak the inside of his boots. Ever. Not even in fun. He dropped his backpack beside Philip's. 'Come on, old fellow,' he said briskly. 'I'm sure Santiago is well satisfied with the demonstration. Philip. Philip!'

They dragged him from the stream unceremoniously, laid him on his back on the bank.

'What's happened? What's the matter with him?'

Philip's eyes were open, staring. There was a trickle of something that looked suspiciously like vomit coming from the corner of his mouth.

'It must be his heart.'

'Could he have had some sort of a stroke?'

'We have to do something.' Rebecca turned Philip's head, used a handkerchief to clean out his mouth. 'Resuscitation,' she said briskly. 'We have to resuscitate him as soon as possible.'

'Do you mean he isn't breathing?' Ella asked uncertainly.

Rebecca gave her a withering glance. 'Anyone know how to do heart massage?' Oliver nodded and between them they began to work on Philip's inert body.

Jonah spread out the pilgrim guide on the bank. 'We're in Lavacolla. There were houses back there. More, I think, than there are ahead. I'll go back and get help.' He left the map where it was and began to run.

After five minutes Rebecca knew she was tiring. 'Could someone take over?' she asked.

Without hesitation Ella said, 'I'll help, if you tell me what to do.'

'I'll take over from Rebecca,' said Oliver. 'Ella, you take over from me. Show her where to put her hands and count for her, Rebecca.'

Ella did her best, but it was clear she was not doing very well and after a few moments Rebecca took over the heart massage again from her. There was no sign of movement, there had been no sign of movement from Philip's body from the moment they had laid him on the bank. Bill said gently. 'I think you should stop now.'

They froze. Bill went to kneel beside Philip. He felt the side of the man's neck, seeking in vain for a pulse. He looked up. 'There is nothing more to do,' he said simply. 'He's dead.' His hand hovered over the face of the man who continued to stare blankly up at them, despite their efforts to revive him, and when he lifted it, Philip's eyes were closed.

Ella made no sound but put her hands up to her mouth as though to stifle the natural, if useless, protest.

But Rebecca declared fiercely, 'You have no right to stop us. How do you know we. . . . There's not been time. . . . If we work on him for longer, something might. . . . There must be some life there, still. Move away. Let me. . . .' Ella, her own eyes fastened on Oliver, shook her head soberly. Oliver stood up, took Rebecca's arm in a gentle hold and drew her to her feet though she continued to struggle, resisting his efforts to guide her away. 'Philip's not dead,' Rebecca cried. 'He can't be.' *He can't be*. Her cry was absorbed by the stream, by the sound of water running over the stones, the leaves on the alders drooping from the bank. As her words died away, the ripple of the water was the only thing left to disturb the silence. 'It's not fair,' and her voice wobbled. 'Philip wanted to get to Compostela so badly. He's walked all this way. We've only got a few miles to go. All those miles, days of walking. How could he die now, this morning?'

'Hush,' said Oliver. Knowing it was not so much Philip's sudden death as that of her children that was distressing her so, he put his arms round Rebecca, drawing her head into his shoulder. 'Ssh.'

Bill was on the point of telling Rebecca harshly to pull herself together when he remembered what Oliver had told him about her babies. So much death in such short a time was enough to unhinge all but the most robust. He said compassionately, 'I think we should say a prayer. There are rituals for the dying, you know, and I have a feeling that Philip would like to see us observing them.'

Rebecca shuddered. Oliver could hear her as if she were shrieking the words, though no sound came from her throat. *Even you are admitting that there might still be life there. How could you not let us go on? If there had been someone – anyone – at the fire maybe Charley and Toby would be here still. We could at least try to save Philip.*

'May I?' Bill looked round the three who remained. It seemed important that they should understand his priestly rôle. 'I am ordained. May I?' When no one objected – in Ella's case through sheer shock – he knelt down by Philip and began softly intoning the rite for the dead.

It seemed too private a moment. Ella walked away and sat by the stream. After a moment Oliver and Rebecca joined her and there the three waited. 'It's too soon for a funeral,' said Oliver, shifting restlessly. 'Why is he doing this?'

'To comfort us, himself. Does it matter? Did you know about Bill?' Ella asked while Bill was praying silently by Philip's body. Oliver shook his head. 'It does explain. . . .'

'Why did he die? How did he die?' Rebecca whispered urgently, oblivious to anything else.

'Some sort of a heart attack, I suppose,' said Ella. 'It must surely have been totally unexpected. He never complained of heart problems, did he?' They shook their heads. 'Ah well. We'll know soon enough.'

'It's not fair.'

Like Bill, Ella was also unsettled by what she considered Rebecca's unseemly reaction. Then she, too, remembered what had happened to her. She shook her head and got up stiffly and walked back to where the body lay. Bill, his mission accomplished, was also getting to his feet.

'I can't bear it,' Rebecca said.

Her words smote Oliver's heart. 'Hush,' he said again. 'Since when has life been anything but life? And you can bear it,' he said, thinking of those two small children. 'You have been so brave. You have borne it, all this time. And I know it's clichéd but it did happen quickly, just like your Charley and Toby. What pain Philip suffered couldn't have been for long, you saw that.'

'But Charley and Toby were too young to suffer anything at all,' Rebecca said stubbornly under her breath.

'I know,' said Oliver hopelessly. 'I don't know how else – what else to say – to comfort you.'

There was a pause. Rebecca fumbled for her handkerchief, wiped her eyes and blew her nose. 'I know,' she replied. Then she added humbly, 'but thank you for trying.'

# Chapter Twenty-Three

The wait for help seemed interminable though it took less than forty minutes for an ambulance crew to reach them with a stretcher and all their equipment. Jonah had knocked on two doors before he had found a phone, but the young woman he discovered hanging up washing in her garden had been very helpful. 'It happens, along the Camino,' she said simply. 'Let us hope your friend recovers.'

'They asked about insurance,' Jonah told Bill in an undertone as the two Spaniards were dealing with the body. 'I said he had it? Though now. . . . I suppose there's no doubt. . . .'

'He's dead. Though I imagine they can't actually pronounce him dead here. As for the insurance, I checked with everyone before we set off. I'd also wondered about bringing a mobile phone. Should we. . . .'

Jonah said, 'The day you want it, the battery's dead. I mean. . . .'

Bill said gently, 'Don't worry. We'll use that word all too frequently, you'll find, and out of context.'

Jonah reached for his backpack. 'I'm going in the ambulance with Philip. How long do you think it'll take you to reach Santiago?'

Bill thought for a moment. 'We were going to have lunch at Monte del Gozo. We'll need to eat a lot sooner than that.'

'I couldn't touch a thing,' said Ella.

'That's shock,' said Bill. 'We'll have to eat to keep our strength up. We don't want anyone else . . . anyone collapsing,' he amended. 'We'll take frequent short breaks today and we still ought to be at the cathedral about five.'

'I'll meet you in the square in front of the cathedral,' said Jonah. 'Oh my God,' he said, appalled. 'Philip told me there was a possibility that Posy would be coming to Santiago to meet him. He said like it was cool she was coming because there'd been a bit of aggro between them recently.'

'Do you want me to come with you, just in case she is there?' asked Oliver.

Jonah shook his head. 'No worries, mate. I'll cope. But thanks for offering,' and there was that in his voice which forbade anyone else from making the same offer.

Bill said awkwardly, 'If there's a single room at the Reyes Católicos, take it. We should stay together until after the funeral.' His words carried. There was a shocked pause. Bill sighed. 'I expect they will release the body for burial in a day or so. If she is here, we can't leave Philip's widow until then.'

'Of course not,' said Ella. 'Go on, Jonah. They are waiting for you. We'll see you this evening.'

'I hope they don't make difficulties about the boy's Compostela,' said Bill.

'What difficulties can they make?' asked Oliver.

'Well, he won't have walked the final day,' answered Bill.

'But he didn't desert his friend,' said Ella. 'I daresay that counts for something.'

No one remembered much about the walk that day. They skirted the end of the runway without so much as lifting their eyes. Bill was scrupulous about stopping every hour and just before two o'clock he took out his own food which he began to eat. It tasted like sawdust. He coaxed Ella all the same. 'Come on, have something, even if it's only an apple.' Dutifully Ella ate her apple. Then she ate a bar of chocolate. 'That's better,' said Bill.

'What'll happen now?' asked Rebecca.

'There'll have to be a pathologist's autopsy,' said Bill. 'Sudden death and all that. If Jonah and the hospital haven't already thought about it, I'll get in touch with Philip's insurance company straight away.'

'And the British Consulate,' said Ella.

'I suppose it's all going to take time,' said Oliver.

'A lot will depend on whether Posy wants the body home for burial,' said Bill, 'or opt for cremation here.'

'You seem to know a great deal about all this,' commented Rebecca.

'I am – was – a parish priest.' It rated hardly as an item of news, still less as a revelation. What had he expected, thought Bill? That they would leap to their feet and cast him forth.

'It's useful to have someone who knows the ropes,' said Oliver.

'Scarcely that,' muttered Bill. 'I've only been on the receiving end, and that was years ago.'

Ella looked as though she might continue the conversation but Oliver was packing his lunch away. 'I can't eat anything else. Maybe later.'

They climbed to the top of Monte del Gozo – the Mount of Joy. 'We need Jonah here to tell us tales of pilgrims of old who wept tears of uncontainable emotion when they looked down on Santiago de Compostela for the first time. I know they usually sang a psalm or a hymn.'

'Philip and I said we'd sing *To Be a Pilgrim*,' said Ella, 'but I don't think I could.'

'I think we should try,' said Bill. In a pleasing baritone he began to sing:

> He who would valiant be
> 'Gainst all disaster,
> Let him in constancy
>    Follow the master.
> There's no discouragement
> Shall make him once relent
> His first avowed intent
>    To be a pilgrim.

Ella joined in after the first couple of lines and Oliver found himself ending the first verse with them. It was Ella who began the second verse:

Who so beset him round
With dismal stories,
Do but themselves confound
   His strength the more is
No foes shall stay his might,
Though he with giants fight:
He will make good his right
   To be a pilgrim.

Halfway through, Ella became choked. Surprisingly, it was Rebecca who added her soprano voice. 'It's amazing what you remember from school,' she muttered in an aside to Ella who smiled a watery smile and began the last verse.

Since, Lord, thou dost defend
Us with thy spirit,
We know we at the end
   Shall life inherit.
Then fancies flee away!
I'll fear not what men say,
I'll labour night and day
   To be a pilgrim.

Rebecca shivered despite the warmth of the day. It was an eerie feeling, singing a half-remembered hymn on the top of a hill under the shadow of a huge monument (which she, personally. thought in execrable taste) erected to honour the visit of Pope John Paul II in 1993. There were ghosts all around, the spirits of the countless thousands who over the centuries had come before – and those who had not made it. A lump rose in her throat. Why, she wondered, was she so upset by this death? After all, Philip, though a friend, was still basically a stranger and most probably would have remained so. Those times when she had visited her little graves had affected her less than this place now. But of course that was not true. She was just more open to sorrow now than she was then. Then she was resisting all emotion. Now she wanted to howl, but maybe Oliver was right and there was no point in railing at life for being what it was. You just had to accept it. It was conceivable that Philip, having got the very best out of his life, was up there, among the ghosts and just willing them to get on with it – and, with more than a touch of whimsy, that Charley and Toby were there, beside him.

'I think we should go and find Jonah, don't you?' she turned and said to the rest.

The milestones had run out; they had reached houses, pavements, shops selling the mundane as well as the tourist tat that might be expected. Each one plodded onwards, head down – thus attracting a few curious stares. Pilgrims were two-a-penny, but usually they looked euphoric. The fleeting and pitying thought was that these must have endured a particularly arduous journey.

They reached a square. They were outside the north façade of the cathedral. *'They sell scallop shells to pilgrims . . .'* muttered Bill.

'What was that?' asked Ella.

'Aymeric Picaud,' he answered, adding wryly, 'Jonah should be here to quote the rest of it.'

They continued down a slope, under an arch, and entered the Plaza del Obradoiro. They had arrived. And there, sitting on a wall outside the Hostal de los Reyes Católicos, his legs stretched out before him, was Jonah. They quickened their pace and went over to greet him.

'How has it been?' asked Ella, giving Jonah a brief hug.

'Philip was pronounced dead on arrival at the hospital and some of the formalities have been completed. You was right about Philip's wife. She arrived last night. I phoned and told her there'd been some sort of an accident.' He shrugged. 'Well, I couldn't tell her over the phone, could I?'

'Poor Jonah. You must have had a dreadful experience,' said Ella.

He continued, 'There's to be a post mortem and Posy has to go back on Monday for the results. I've checked into the hotel and told them you were on your way.' He hesitated: 'Posy wants to have dinner with us. I guess we just support her as best we can.'

'Of course we must,' said Ella gently.

'Shall we go into the cathedral now?' asked Bill. 'Before we go to the hotel?'

Rebecca was about to say she was dying for a shower (that word again) then she thought better of it anyway. 'I suppose pilgrims do this part in their dishevelled state.'

'You don't look dishevelled,' said Oliver, 'a little weary, but you're entitled.'

They climbed the steep steps together to the west door then they joined the small queue inside, round the Tree of Jesse, carved on the central column of the doorway leading to one of the aisles. Over this was a seated St James in pilgrim garb, smiling a welcome. Traditionally pilgrims touched the Tree of Jesse in thanksgiving for a safe arrival and bearing witness to this ritual were five deeply indented finger marks at chest height. On the other side of the column was a carving of the architect, Master Mateo, and to this Ella pushed Jonah. 'Go on,' she said, 'it's too late for me, but you have all your intellectual life ahead of you. Knock your forehead against him and he'll endow you with wisdom.'

'Hey,' protested Jonah, 'who's supposed to be the storyteller in this party, you or me?' But they noticed he carried out the ritual, all the same.

They queued to climb behind the high altar to embrace the statue of St James and leave the stones at his feet which they had carried since the first day. 'But did you notice the little monk sitting beside it was sweeping them away as soon as our backs were turned?' whispered Ella to Oliver as the queue now snaked its way down to the crypt to file past the tomb of the Apostle. Oliver grinned wryly.

They emerged once again into the light of early evening. 'What next?' asked Rebecca.

'I'm going to find the office and collect my Compostela,' said Bill. 'Are you coming with me?'

'I'll come,' said Ella slowly, 'though I'm still not sure . . . and there were all those bus rides. . . .'

'I'll come with you,' said Jonah, unexpectedly. 'Just in case the priest doesn't speak English.'

Oliver said, 'Might as well, I suppose.'

'No,' said Rebecca firmly. 'I'll have my passport stamped at the hotel. I did what I had to do, but the Compostela isn't for me. It'll look just as good when I have it framed. I'll see you later in the bar.' It had all become overwhelming, too much emotion, their arrival. She wanted a long wallow in a hot bath surrounded by five star luxury while she indulged herself in a small weep.

'Ooh, look, a genuine pilgrim,' a heavily-accented voice said. 'May we photograph you, please?'

Rebecca turned, bemused. Erupting from a coach was a large group of Japanese tourists, chattering animatedly. She caught the words, 'Pilgrim', and 'Photograph'. *God*, she thought, *my hair's a mess and I've no lipstick and they want to photograph me. Tourists!*

But half-laughing, half-crying, she permitted herself to be posed against the background of the Hostal de los Reyes Católicos, the pilgrims' hospital founded in 1492 after the reconquest of Granada, while forty or more cameras clicked. 'Thank you, thank you,' they said, smiling and bowing, and she bowed in turn and smiled at the absurdity of it all.

Meanwhile the others had found the Oficina de Acogida del Peregrino in the Dean's House and joined another small queue that was moving very slowly. A pilgrim emerged looking pale and stunned. 'It's like the Inquisition,' he told them. 'What were my motives, did I really walk more than two hundred kilometres?'

'But did you get your Compostela?'

He waved it at them and clattered down the uncarpeted and polished wooden stairs.

'I've just realized what that pile of wood in the foyer is,' said Ella soberly. 'I thought it was a pile of firewood. It's pilgrims' staves.'

Bill said, 'Pilgrims leave their staves here in thanksgiving since they won't be needing them any more.'

'Jonah cut me mine. On that very first day when he joined us. I'm not leaving that behind.' There was a pause. Ella hovered uncertainly. She stared at the young people queuing ahead of them, cyclists by their clothing. They all looked so earnest, so – so idealistic. She remembered her feelings in the cathedral, firstly immense thankfulness that she had accomplished the journey, intense sadness that Philip had not, awe at the splendour that surrounded them and dismay – revulsion even – at some of the trappings that came with the ending of the pilgrimage. She would have liked to have asked Philip how he felt, embracing the gilded saint. . . . She turned back to the others abruptly. 'This isn't for me,' she said. 'I'll see you tonight.'

The priest in charge of their interrogation spoke excellent English. He was also extremely sympathetic when Bill told him about Philip's sudden death. 'There was a Welshman, Guillaum Watt, who died close to Santiago de Compostela in 1993.'

'I remember seeing that memorial,' said Bill. 'He was sixty-nine. So poignant.'

'Yet who is to say either man did not die in a state of grace.'

Bill emerged smiling from his interview which had lasted longer than most but there was that in his face that forbade probing. He was also holding his Compostela as though it was made of the finest spun gold. 'I was asked especially if we would all be at the pilgrim mass tomorrow. I said we would. Was I right?' he asked anxiously.

Jonah noticed the diffidence. That was new. 'I am sure you are,' he said. 'We'll tell everyone tonight what he said.'

'You next?'

'I've decided I'll walk the final stretch first. It won't be difficult to hitch a lift to Lavacolla and walk from there.'

Oliver, too, came out with his Compostela. He seemed pleased. 'I don't think I'll be going quite to the extreme of having this framed,' he said, 'but it makes for a good souvenir, doesn't it.'

'Yes, you old cynic,' said Bill affectionately, 'it most certainly does.'

There was a moment's awkwardness when they all met in the bar that evening to find Posy already there with Jonah, a woman they had not seen since their first meeting in London. Philip had been reticent about his marriage. They had taken this to mean merely that she had declined to make the pilgrimage – nothing more. They found her drawn, but composed. 'Thank you,' she said simply, 'for being with Philip. It would have been a great comfort to him.'

She had the grace not to apologize for being a dampener on their achievement.

It was over the vieiras de Santiago, scallops, that Jonah made his suggestion. 'I've Posy's permission to mention this,' he said, intercepting a nod from her. 'You see, when we were given Philip's effects at the hospital, they had found a piece of paper in one of his pockets. It was a poem. I've had it duplicated.' He passed a sheet of paper to each one of them.

'Apparently Philip has been writing poetry on the pilgrimage,' his widow said. 'I knew he was keeping notes of the journey but in the back of his notebook are several attempts at poetry. I think this must have been the one he most liked.'

'I think it would be a good idea if we arranged for a memorial stone to be erected at Lavacolla,' said Jonah, 'inscribed with his name, the dates, and this poem.'

'I like this,' said Oliver. He quoted, '*Was it for this he'd drawn near, His soul's salvation?*'

'But you can't separate the final two lines without destroying the meaning of the whole poem,' objected Bill. 'It omits all the effort that went into the pilgrimage – even the effort that went into the writing of the poem.'

'I think it's a beautiful epitaph,' said Ella. 'Let's do it.'

'Yes.' The decision came readily, unanimously.

'Could we meet in a year, the anniversary of his death, and dedicate it?'

Rebecca looked at Posy. It seemed so insensitive to be discussing the anniversary of her husband's death before he was even buried. 'He'd like that. I'd like that,' Posy said. 'Nobody knows – I'd like to believe not even Philip – but when he left on this trip I fully intended leaving him. Somehow, over the weeks, I began having second thoughts. That's why I came. Silly man, to die before I got here.' There was a shocked silence before they noticed Posy was smiling though her eyes were large with unshed tears. 'I'd like to celebrate his anniversary and I don't expect you to drop your plans and come back home for his funeral. I'm sure Philip would hate the very idea of that, but the other . . . that's good. As many of us as possible to be there, at Lavacolla, on the day he died, next year.'

# Chapter Twenty-Four

Pilgrim mass was another emotional event. There must have been at least two hundred pilgrims packed into the centre aisle of the cathedral that Saturday morning, the officiating priest declaring before he began that only those who had made the pilgrimage were welcome. Then he told the congregation of Philip's sudden death and asked for their prayers. Sitting with them, Posy wept, the tears rolling unchecked down her cheeks. No matter that recently the quality of their relationship had deteriorated, Philip had been her husband for many years. It seemed to her that there was sufficient affection still there for them to have built on it when they returned home, to have become loving companions, mutually supportive. It was a cruel ending to a long life together, and she sat hunched into herself on the wooden pew and just prayed it would all go away.

But the pilgrim mass was a joyous event, for most. Bill was euphoric. He felt humble, cleansed, positive about his future. He was going to see Father Jerome as soon as possible and he hoped a forgiving church would receive him into its bosom with open arms.

Ella was simply relieved it was all over. As the botafumeiro, the immense silver censer, was swung by no less than eight tiraboleiros at the end of the service, the sense of circus made her long once more for the matter-of-factness of Philip. Standing next to Posy, she took the widow's hand and squeezed it. It would be a worthy pilgrimage to return next year. Maybe by then she might have come to understand this one. Now? Well, now she was looking forward to going home, to gathering round her just those things that meant most to her and to ending her life in peace. Had she really meant to go on travelling? Probably not, though it maybe depended on how quickly she regained her strength.

Oliver, by contrast, was more unsettled than at any time since they had all started the journey. It was true the next few days were to be filled purposefully – he and Jonah were to visit a stonemason on the Monday, then he and Rebecca were to undertake an extensive programme of sightseeing. There were certain curiosities he had read about, a balustrade with pre-Columbian motifs which he wanted to find and in the church of Santa María a baroque altar with little sculpted angels wearing glasses. Then there would be the moment of farewells. It was afterwards that loomed as one enormous blank. So much for the pilgrimage that was supposed to give his life a reason. There was neither reason nor purpose anywhere in the days ahead. He had absolutely no idea what to do next.

Rebecca had definite plans. The first of these involved shopping. It was one thing to make her first appearance at the Reyes Católicos in pilgrim garb, to come to mass that morning in clean, if worn pilgrim clothes. It was quite another to endure a day more than she had to of shabbiness. Then there was sightseeing with Oliver. She was looking forward to that. After that, she had decided she would go home and sort out her ticket to New Zealand. Charley and Toby would be forever in her heart. There was no need to remain close to that piece of earth where they lay. Yet, and she shifted uneasily on the hard pew, there was something missing. She had not expected to feel like this at the end of the journey. Something not quite right about. . . . But the congregation rose to its feet, there was that rustle of anticipation and the united gasp as the botafumeiro swung from side to side of the crossing until it almost touched the roof, glowing fiercely as it descended, leaving a billowing trail of fragrant smoke behind it like a heavenly comet.

And then they were in the square and the pilgrimage was over.

It took a week before the formalities were completed. There was a lengthy telephone conversation between Posy and James, which became heated when tentatively she suggested bringing back Philip's ashes after cremation in Spain.

'Like hand luggage. Mother, you're joking.'

When James called her Mother he was at his most disapproving. 'In some ways the formalities are easier,' she said weakly.

'A former churchwarden. It's hardly suitable, Mother.'

Weakly she allowed herself to be overridden, this time. But instead of abandoning herself to her intense grief which instinct told her to, Posy stiffened her back and made resolutions that were to have considerable repercussions in the affairs of the young people who were only waiting for her return (with or without their living father) to lay at her feet all the trials and tribulations the world had fashioned especially for them. Yet, oh, she would miss him so for instinct also persuaded her that there would have been sufficient compromise for them to have lived together in harmony. If only. . . . She would miss the warmth of another body in the bed, the knowledge that there was at least one other person in the world to whom she mattered – for whatever reason. Posy wondered how she would cope with the loneliness of it all.

Jonah said he'd hitch to Lavacolla the day after the visit to the stonemason. Bill offered to accompany him but Jonah declined, saying the day on his own was something he needed, if only to sort out in his mind his next plans. So many of them still unsure of what to do next. . . . Bill nodded affably and said he'd see him at dinner.

Oliver, still restless, had another idea. He suggested to Rebecca that they hired a car and drove to Orca, some twenty-five kilometres to the south of Santiago. 'There's a garden I'd like to visit. They say the terraces are covered with rust-coloured lichen, there's a water lily pool and a stone boat floating on a lake.'

'Very Santiagoish,' she said.

'What?'

'The stone boat. St James's boat was supposed to have been stone. Remember?'

'I'd forgotten.' There was that in his face and tone of voice that suggested there was a great deal he had not forgotten.

Rebecca found herself blushing faintly – at her age – as she replied, 'It sounds idyllic.'

To Oliver's surprise Rebecca was still wearing the clothes she had worn on the journey when they met after breakfast, clean though they were and pressed, but shabby. The day and the garden was all that he had promised. It was pleasantly warm but not hot. There were other people in the garden, but by chance it felt as though they had the place to themselves. The vistas were charming and the lake Arthurian – or Santiagoish – that was the only thing over which they could not agree.

They were sitting in companionable silence by the lake in the shade cast by dark shrubs. 'Toby would have loved that boat,' Rebecca said. 'But I can hear Charley protesting that it would be stupid to sail in a stone boat. She was always a realist.'

Oliver took her hand. 'Do you know this is the first time I've heard you speak of the children light-heartedly?' Almost he had not said it, fearing to upset her.

Rebecca thought for a moment. 'You're right. And do you know why? It was listening to Posy last night. For the first time I recognized that I'm not unique.' Oliver squeezed her hand and she laughed. It was a little unsteady, but it was a laugh. 'You know what I mean. I shall never, ever, not think of them daily, but I truly do realize that I'm not the only one with a tragedy to bear. It's taken a long time. . . .'

'It was meant to.'

'That's a novel idea,' she said, digesting it. Another plan that had come into her mind coalesced. 'I'm going to walk to *Finis Terrae* before I go home,' she announced.

Oliver felt as though his heart had been given a sudden jolt. 'Whatever for?' he exclaimed. 'Only the other day you were insisting you'd never walk another step unless you had to.'

'I feel as if my journey isn't over yet. Santiago was only the finish of part of it. I want to see this mystical end of the earth, the edge of the western world you get to before you fall off.'

'Invoking the ancients? You'll be telling me you'll be making burnt offerings next.'

She smiled. 'I have a hankering to burn my stinking pilgrim clothes on the sand, wash myself in the Atlantic and dress in totally new things to symbolize it's really all over,' she admitted. 'Does it sound so very far-fetched?'

'I don't suppose the local council'll be much in favour of a load of pilgrims despoiling their pristine beaches. And the Atlantic'll probably be freezing,' he added repressively.

'I expect it will,' she agreed amicably. 'One woman is not exactly a load of pilgrims, though.'

'So when are you going to do this sub-pilgrimage?'

'As soon as we see Posy and – and Philip off. I didn't book a flight yesterday. I didn't even go shopping while you were at the stonemason. I just sat in the square and watched the crowds. Now I know why. I don't suppose it'll take more than a few days and I'm sure there'll be transport back. I'll buy a skirt or something to wear for when it's over. I'll see if the hotel has a room. If not,' she shrugged.

Oliver got up abruptly. 'It's time we went,' he said stiffly. 'If we don't go soon we'll be late for dinner.' They always dined late. It was an absurd excuse. Rebecca followed him. She seemed oblivious to his feelings of absolute rejection, total hurt. How stupid he was being, Oliver thought savagely, positively childish. He should have known better. There never had been a question of any sort of relationship developing between them. Once or twice since the mugging he'd wondered. But now. . . . Walking to Finisterre was the last thing he wanted to do, that was for sure. Though she might at least have asked him, even if only for politeness' sake.

Rebecca was indeed oblivious to Oliver's seething emotions. She was more than a little wounded by the way he had scoffed at her intention, bruised by his so patent scorn. Once, not so very long ago, she had thought he could be the one to fill the empty spaces of her heart. Now? Now she would have liked to suggest he came with her, but it was impossible to do any such thing, even if it was only for the sake of companionship. She did not really want to walk all that way on her own and having Oliver beside her would have been a promise of. . . . Of what? The beginning of a serious relationship, she admitted with total honesty, which might not lead anywhere, but she wanted nothing more. She definitely wanted to finish this journey properly. Still, if that was what Oliver thought of her, it was surely better to know it now. She lifted her chin and walked ahead of him to where their car was parked.

Oliver saw the little gesture and unconsciously repeated it. If that was what she wanted, so be it. They scarcely exchanged a word on the way back. It was a disastrous end to an expedition that had started so well.

At the airport Ella and Bill took charge of the formalities for Posy who, desperately needing the comfort of her family, seemed incapable of making decisions. Ella took hold of Posy's hand as they waited for their gate to be put up on the board and squeezed it. 'It's all right. You're not alone. Bill and I are here.'

'Where's Jonah?' Bill asked. They had not seen him since the previous evening.

'Isn't that him over there,' Ella craned her neck. 'I thought . . . but no, it doesn't look like him at all. I never saw Jonah dressed in brown.'

'He said his farewells to me last night,' said Posy, making an effort. 'Told me he couldn't abide the thought of standing on one foot while they loaded Philip into the hold.'

'Idiot boy. I wanted to . . . oh, well.'

Bill began to snort, 'Really, the manners of. . . .' Then his voice tailed away. 'He's been such a good friend. To us all. I'd have liked. . . .'

'He'll be here, next year,' predicted Posy.

Rebecca turned from Bill, who had hugged her unselfconsciously, to hold Posy closely to her. 'I won't forget Philip,' she promised. 'Send you a postcard from New Zealand.'

'And I shall be at Lavacolla, from wherever I am,' said Oliver, hugging first Posy, then Ella. 'Bye, Ella.'

'Be sure you write to me.'

'I will.'

' 'Bye.'

It had been Jonah. He smiled benignly, a distant, enigmatic figure in brown, nodding in turn towards each one of the companions. Then he picked up his staff and was gone.

'What now?' Oliver, hovering, spoke to Rebecca for the first time that morning.

'I've left my backpack at the hotel. I didn't think it was cheating, coming here without it. I thought I'd start my last journey from the square.'

'Your last journey?'

'Don't sound so horrified. I am coming back from *Finis Terrae*. You know what I meant, the last phase of this journey. Before I. . . . Well, before I go to New Zealand. And that probably means I shan't be at Lavacolla this time next year. I certainly am unlikely to be able to afford the fare to Europe quite so soon. Which means, goodbye Oliver.' Their eyes locked but the barrier remained firmly in place and neither would permit the other to see how desperately each wanted it to be breached to allow a glimpse of a needy soul behind it. She stood there uncertainly, not sure whether to hold out her hand, embrace him spontaneously – which would be difficult since that particular gesture would be utterly unspontaneous having been rehearsed in her mind and desired for so long – or what.

The others had gone. She was the only one left. Ice, a protective carapace of obstinacy, a refusal to parade deeply buried emotions that might otherwise be scraped raw by her, suddenly broke. He cracked, croaked, 'Rebecca.'

It was not a second too soon. Her moment of hesitation had passed. She had already turned to go.

'Rebecca.'

Had she heard her name? It was repeated louder. She turned back.

This time Oliver would not meet her gaze. His head slightly to one side, his eyes examining the toes of his dusty trainers, he said, 'I can't wear these for much longer. They really need to be slung on a bonfire.' Then he looked at her squarely and asked simply, 'Do you think I might come to *Finis Terrae* with you?'

# Acknowledgements

I consulted frequently *A Practical Guide for Pilgrims: The Road to Santiago* by Millán Bravo Lozano, published by Editorial Everest, S.A., and many of Jonah's stories appear there. Others were told us during water-stops on a supported journey by Harriet from ATG. *The Song (Chanson) of Roland* is A.E. Way's rendering quoted in Brewer's *Dictionary of Phrase and Fable*, Centenary Edition, 1977. *He Who Would Valiant Be* is from *The English Hymnal with Tunes*, Geoffrey Cumberlege, Oxford University Press, London, E.C. A.R. Mowbray & Co., Ltd., 1933. The quotation by Nicholas Luard comes from *The Field of the Star*, published by Michael Joseph, 1998.